Circles of Blue

Bizarre Tales
by
D. E. Graham

PublishAmerica
Baltimore

ISBN: 1-4137-2534-1
PUBLISHED BY PUBLISHAMERICA, LLLP
www.publishamerica.com
Baltimore

Printed in the United States of America

Table of Contents

Circles of Blue   7

The Lamp   17

The Guardian   22

Dream House   27

Trucking   33

Once in a Lifetime   39

The Breaking Point   45

End of the Line   52

The Light   58

The Deep Sleep   61

Happy   67

Dead Wrong   71

This book is dedicated to my three daughters: Darla, Rochelle, and Carrie; being my first critics, they sat for endless hours and listened to my stories. And also to my late husband, Bud, who kept me motivated.

Had it not been for Sun , Margaret, the women of the Fifties- Plus chat room, and the women I work with, I would never have had the courage to allow others to see my writings. These people gave me the encouragement I needed to finish my book and submit it. Thank you, Ladies, for your input on my future as an author.

Circles of Blue

When Jimmy Joe Callister left town suddenly back in June of 1963, nobody seemed the least bit surprised or concerned. This wasn't the first time he had taken off without letting anyone know where he was going. No one really cared when he would disappear on his little escapades, and these were the only times when nobody was bothered by his unwanted presence.

Jimmy Joe was known for being the town bully. Even as a boy and teenager—being overgrown for his age, he managed to bully a lot of the town's people, and even more so—his aging parents. His parents had prayed for the day when he would turn of age, hoping he would move out and into his own place, leaving them alone. They found their prayers to have been in vain, however, because he didn't move. He had it made living off of them and he knew it. He was too lazy to make it for himself, and enjoyed having someone wait on him hand and foot. He sponged off them for several years and what they wouldn't give him willingly—he managed to get with his threats, or by stealing it. They lived in total chaos, and only when they passed away in September, did he finally look for work.

Their deaths—being within two days of each other, were questioned by the town authorities. However, the results were clear that they had both died of heart failure, which cleared Jimmy Joe of all suspicions. Even so, this didn't stop the whispers behind his back and the talk among people in local gatherings. Everyone had known the terrible way he had treated his parents.

"Even if they did die from heart attacks, he probably caused them." I overheard a woman talking to a cashier at a fast food restaurant. Even though I thought the same thing—because of my job being in public service, I knew it was best to keep my opinion to myself.

Jimmy Joe never lasted long on any job. He usually got himself canned for his missing or slacking of work. He also had a knack for starting fights, which were usually one-sided; being the brute he was, nobody wanted to fight with him. However, once after taking a jab at a foreman who had jumped him for laying down on the job, it was a shock to Jimmy Joe when the foreman came back at him with a blow of his own, knocking him off his feet, leaving him sitting on the floor holding his jaw. It was something he hadn't anticipated. After that incident, he watched his actions around certain people and the town also seemed to change their attitude about what they would or wouldn't allow Jimmy Joe to get away with.

Because he lacked friends and had very few acquaintances, he chose to go out of town to places he wasn't known, in order to find temporary companionship. So when he left town that day in June, nobody paid much attention. It was just another one of his foolish excursions. It was only when he returned two weeks later that people started talking.

The talk around town was, "hey, have you seen Jimmy Joe since he got back?" Everywhere you went someone was talking. "He pulled through town yesterday with this young girl in the car," I overheard a man saying to a cashier at the grocery. "Man, I do mean young. She couldn't have been more than thirteen or fourteen years old. I guess he really went and robbed the cradle this time. Either that or he's done gone and added kidnapping to the rest of the stuff he's done."

The day after Jimmy Joe returned to town, he started his habitual rounds of the local bars, and everyone heard the story they had eagerly been waiting for. Jimmy Joe had gotten married.

"Yeah, she's young. And she's kind of dumb," Jimmy Joe gloated as he sat mooching drinks from those who wanted to hear. "That's how I like them though: young and dumb. You see, that way you keep control. I don't want no woman telling me when I can come or go, or how to run things around my own house. Nope, ain't gonna happen. You gotta get them when they're young and dumb like she is. See, that way you can train them to do what *you* want them to do, not what *they* want. And you gotta put some fear in them too. See, that way they're afraid not to do what you tell them!"

"Hey where'd you ever find her at, Jimmy Joe?" One guy asked as he stared into his drink. He hated giving Jimmy Joe the time of day, let alone ask him anything, but the curiosity had gotten the best of him.

"She's from Coldwater. That's about a hundred miles from here. You heard of it ain't you?" He asked, slopping down the drinks as fast as they could sit them on the bar. He knew the novelty of the situation would soon fade, and after everyone learned all they wanted to know, the drinks would stop coming. "It's a little burg just south of here," he said, answering himself. "I've been seeing her on and off now for about two, three months. Her folks were glad to get her married off, because they got seven more of them at home."

The talk of Jimmy Joe's wife soon died down. Since she wasn't seen around town, most people figured she had left and gone back to where she came from, not being able to put up with the likes of a bully like Jimmy Joe.

Jimmy Joe's house sat back a long lane on the outskirts of town. It was fairly secluded being surrounded by a cluster of trees and overgrown brush, with only a small part of the roof remaining visible from the road. Jimmy Joe never had visitors because he had no friends, and his only known relatives had been his parents. Now that they were gone, no one would waste the time or take the effort required to make their way down his unkempt lane to visit the likes of him. He frequented the local bars, always drinking as much as the money he had on him would allow. Sometimes in a drunken stupor, he would brag about the little woman he had waiting faithfully at home for him. Most everyone would shrug it off, thinking he was trying to save face by not telling the truth about her leaving him. The day came however, when to everyone's surprise, Jimmy Joe rushed his wife to the local hospital to give birth.

The talk around town was rekindled by the nurses who had been on duty when he had arrived. They spoke about a backward young girl named Jenny, who had been afraid to talk to anyone except Jimmy Joe. After she gave birth to her son and was in a quiet room away from Jimmy Joe, they were able to coax her into opening up a little. She told them she had come from a small backwoods community; and being one of eight children, her parents had welcomed the opportunity of her being taken off their hands, even though she had only been fourteen at the time.

"Mama said she was fourteen when she got married and it didn't hurt her none", she said as her ignorance shone through her soft saddened eyes. "Jimmy Joe said he could give me the things they couldn't." From what they could make out, Jimmy Joe had done a real song and dance on her parents, bragging about his land and his nice large house. But even with his house in the dilapidated condition that it was in—if they had seen it, they would have thought it to be a mansion, as compared to the living conditions they were used to. He had her so brainwashed and so wrapped up in him, it would have taken years of counseling to pull her free. The nurses knowing this, wrote her off as being a lost cause and a waste of their time.

Having a child at home didn't slow Jimmy Joe down from his constant barroom trips, although it was getting harder to keep the cash flow he needed, being the worker he wasn't. He became more of a nuisance than he was before, constantly sponging drinks off of whomever he could catch off guard. The ones that were afraid to tell him no, changed their place of converge thinking that would solve their problem, but eventually he would show up there too. Whenever anyone would mention the baby, he would simply reply, "what good are they? All they want to do is cry and eat you out of house and home." From this they could see that being a father wasn't what Jimmy Joe had looked forward to, even though the following year and the next three years after that, like clockwork, Jimmy Joe returned to the hospital for the birth of his and Jenny's Children.

The bills were mounting up for Jimmy Joe. Due to the increase in his family and his outrageous drinking habit, he had swiftly obliterated the huge savings his parents had left him, and had taken to constantly hauling pieces of furniture or odds and ends to the local flea market, in order to turn a fast buck. More recent, he had begun selling off small parcels of his land to keep things going. From time to time, he would even look for work; while he didn't really want a job, he knew it made him look good to let people think he was trying. But money or no money, he still managed to make his way around the bars. His temper would burst in a fiery rage whenever anyone would occasionally mention Jenny or the kids. "I came in here to forget about that bunch!" he snapped, snarling through his yellow, gritted teeth. "So don't you mention them again!"

Early in September, he abruptly stopped making his daily rounds of the bars. The talk started up. It was unbelievable. He hadn't been seen in over a week. At all the local establishments, the joking greeting became: "Have you seen Jimmy Joe around lately?" Some people thought that maybe he had finally seen the light. Maybe Jenny had threatened to leave him, or maybe he had seen where he was doing wrong, wasting all his money on beer, and had finally decided to settle down and make a go of it for Jenny and his kids. But there were others who thought he had just ran out of funds to keep him going. The talk, however, was quick to die down though, because the only concern anyone had about Jimmy Joe's disappearance was the relief they felt by not having to tolerate his unbecoming personality. His disappearance truly was a good riddance.

The thought of Jimmy Joe's disappearance would probably never have occurred to me, if it hadn't been for little Johnny, Jimmy Joe's first born, who had recently turned five. The problem was he hadn't registered for school. Two weeks into the new school year, I was contacted about the situation. I work for the Department of Children's Welfare.

As much as I dreaded the idea of having to face this bully who had no working telephone, I knew I had no other choice but to drive to their home to talk to them about the situation. Pulling up the drive from the road was a task in itself. Parts of the driveway were over-grown with brush, while other parts of it were washed away, leaving stops and potholes all the way to the house. The house itself had an eerie abandoned look. All my wiser instincts were telling me to get the hell out of there, but the dependability of my job forced me to stay.

I stood staring at the peeling paint on the dirty door, as I faintly knocked. *Who knows*, I thought, *maybe no one would be home. Maybe they moved. Maybe* … The door opened slightly. The thin tired face of a young woman peered through the cracked opening. I stood staring unconsciously at the lifeless face that appeared in the doorway before me. The girl looked a good fifteen to twenty years older than she should have. Could living with the likes of Jimmy Joe have caused these age lines on her face, and the void which shadowed her hallowed eyes? Her expression changed slightly, awakening me back to my reason for being there. "I'm … a," I said nervously, stuttering, which was so unlike me. "I'm … a … here to see you about Johnny."

"Why? What's he done?" she asked as her eyes grew wide with anticipation.

"Nothing, nothing at all," I said, trying to calm the disturbed look on her face. "I'm only here with concern about his schooling." She pushed the door open a little wider as she stared at me.

"What do you mean, *his schooling?*" I carefully stepped backward, fearing she might take a wild lunge at me, her tone not being as inviting as what I was used to in the past with other home visits.

"You see," I said, groping for an explanation she would understand. "He should have started school this year. He's five now, isn't he?" She hesitated; her expression seemed to relax a little as she looked me over.

"Yeah, he's five." Her words were blunt and firm, but her expression indicated a cloud of uncertainty.

"Well," I continued, "he should have been registered for school since he's five."

"I don't know about them things," she said. "Jimmy Joe always took care of that stuff. He didn't tell me nothing about no school."

"Well could I see Jimmy Joe then? Maybe it would be better if I was to talk to him." I could see a hint of fear sheathing the uncertainty in her eyes.

"No … no, couldn't do that." Her answer was quick. Her voice was almost a whisper.

"Well, could I come in and talk to you then?" I said trying to keep a pleasant tone to my voice, hoping to calm her uneasiness. "I really need to see the other children too, while I'm here. You see, I'm with the child welfare program, and I have to make a full report on the well being of all the children."

"Why?" She looked more puzzled than before. "They don't all have to go to school. They ain't old enough."

"No, I know they're not old enough for school. This is just procedure. I do it at all the homes I have to visit."

"Well, I guess it'll be alright, if it's what you gotta do." She opened the door wider, standing to the side to allow me to enter.

The house was spacious with very little furniture, but very clean. It gave the appearance of being uninhabited, except for the whispered murmuring I heard coming from an adjoining room. *Must be the kids,* I thought, as I stood eyeing the large opened doorway leading to the next room. I turned to face Jenny who was standing silently behind me. "I really should see Jimmy too," I said. "Is he home now?"

Her expression was the same as before, vagueness, with a hint of fear filling her drained eyes. "No," She whispered. "He ain't here."

"Do you know when he will be here? I would rather talk to the both of you together. I can come back."

"No … He won't … I mean … I don't know." She was becoming extremely nervous and confused.

Maybe he's left her, I thought. It *would* be like Jimmy Joe to take off and leave her alone with these kids without any way to take care of them. "Do you know where he went or where he's at?" I asked not wanting to come right out and ask bluntly if he left her.

"Yeah … I mean no … I mean … a … well … a … It's kinda hard to explain." I could tell something was really troubling her now. She needed desperately to talk to someone. All these years being alone in this house with no contact with the world outside had made her shy toward other people, but now being forced to face another woman, her solitude was diminishing. She had an uncontrollable desire to talk to someone. She had to talk to someone. Now!

I reached out and patted her shoulder. "It's alright," I said calmly. "I'm here to listen." I could see a sudden change in her. She seemed a lot calmer but the frightened look was still present in her eyes. *What had this man done to this child*, I thought, *to put such a fear in her? What kind of a life had she been forced to live at the hands of this drunken bully?*

"Well, you see," she began in a voice that sounded like a whimpering child, interrupting my thoughts. "It was the circles of blue."

Now I was puzzled. "Circles of blue? I'm sorry. I don't know what you mean by circles of blue." I said hoping she would continue. "What is it?"

"Come here. I'll show you," she said, heading for the stairway, motioning for me to follow. She climbed the stairs slowly with me trailing behind her. I felt uneasy about the whole thing and my gut feeling was to turn and get the hell out of that place, but my curiosity kept me climbing. At the top of the stairs she walked over and opened a door and entered with me right behind her. The room was vacant, except for a small cot in one corner pushed against the wall.

"There," she said pointing at the freshly painted white wall, where someone had noticeably drawn several small circles in blue crayon. "See," she continued, "after I got done painting this room I caught Johnny up here drawing with his crayons, these circles of blue. So I asked him why? Why would he want to mess up my nice wall that I worked so hard on, with them circles of blue? And you know what he says?" It was more of a lead than a question, but I shook my head so she would continue with her story. "He says, 'but momma, you let daddy mess up your face with circles of blue. Why should these circles bother you when you don't do anything about the ones he puts on you?' Then I knew the beatings I was getting from Jimmy Joe was messing me up like this here wall, and my kids was seeing what was happening, even though I thought they never seen nothing." She walked over to the cot and sat down, rubbing her face in her hands. I could see she was close to tears so I walked over and sat down beside her, putting my arm around her to help ease her pain.

"Person only wants what's best for their kids, you know. I never wanted them to know about things like that, you see." She looked at me as if for approval, so I nodded my head. I could see the tears in her eyes wanting to flow, but she held them back as she continued to speak. "So anyways, when Jimmy Joe came home that night, drunk as usual, I just flat told him that things were going to change round here 'cause the kids were noticing more, and he was going to have to stop putting the blue marks on me. He was going to have to stop hitting me, 'cause I ain't no wall to be marked on. You know what he said?" The tears gave way and started running down her cheeks as she spoke. I tightened my arm that was around her shoulder, giving her a comforting squeeze.

"What did he say?" I asked, breaking my silence.

"He said I wasn't nothing except what he wanted me to be, and if he felt like hitting me, he would. And as long as he was the one putting the food on the table, I had no say-so what-so-ever. Then he hit me and knocked me against the wall. He was laughing at me and dropped his beer. He bent down to pick it up, still laughing at me. But what he didn't see was Johnny's bat leaning against the wall he knocked me into. So I got up and picked up the bat. When he straightened up, I let him have it. One swing aside his head. He went down like a rag doll and just laid there. I stood over him, waiting and watching, holding the bat in my hand, wanting him to get back up, so I could give it to him again. I thought this would teach him a lesson, giving him a taste of his own medicine. But he didn't get up. And I just stood there watching him for the longest time, just staring and thinking, thinking about how he looked like a big fat overgrown hog lying there on that floor. You know, the more I looked at him the more I thought of him as a hog. I began to picture him all dressed out. You see, I used to help my daddy butcher the hogs when I was at home, before Jimmy Joe came around telling us all lies. That's what they were you know, just lies; lies about how good a life he could give me; lies about how I would never have to want for nothing; lies about how well off our young- uns were going to be.

Well I took about all those lies I could swallow. So when I started thinking about how he would look all dressed out, I thought about one lie he told me I was going to make true, of how he was going to put food on the table. It had been a long time since he had bought any real groceries, and it was hard hearing the kids always saying they were hungry. I mean what can you do when you got nothing to do with? So I drug that fat hog down the steps and on down to the basement, and I dressed him out real good. I know it sounds bad, but he didn't give me much choice, and besides he was already dead. At least the kids got fed. Well I guess it's over now. If only I had known enough to register Johnny for school. But I guess with me being behind in things, you know, being slow and all, I guess things were bound to catch up with me. Right?"

I didn't answer. I was still in shock by what she had told me. I sat staring at the wall with the little blue circles drawn on it. What was going to happen to this girl, this young girl with her babies who wasn't much more than a child herself? What was going to happen to them? Everyone knew that Jimmy Joe was worthless. Everyone knew what a bully he was. He had bullied his parents and the people in the town, and now this girl. He had taken her away from her home and family and brought her to a strange place with strange people, only to be mistreated and bullied over. It wasn't right. It just wasn't right! Jimmy Joe had gotten what he deserved. It was a wonder it hadn't happened sooner. It just wasn't right that this girl and her kids should have to suffer any further. I knew if I told, people were going to look at her as if she was an animal. I knew she wasn't an animal. She was just a helpless child who wasn't capable of hurting anyone, unless to defend herself; and it had taken years of abuse before she had finally gotten the strength to fight back. This had taken real courage on her behalf and I damn sure wasn't going to be the one to destroy that courage. I wasn't going to be the one to judge what she had done, or give anyone else the opportunity. I couldn't begin to imagine what I would have done if I'd been placed in the same situation. How could anyone? How could anyone really know what they would do?

"Momma?" The small inquisitive voice of a child interrupted my thoughts. Johnny stood peering through the open doorway at his mother. "Momma, when we gonna eat?"

"Just a minute, Johnny," she said motioning him away from the door. "You wait downstairs. We'll be right down." She looked at me as she wiped the tears from her streaked face. "You care if I feed my kids first before you take me away?"

"Come on," I said, smiling at her as I followed Johnny down the stairs to the dining room.

The children were all seated around the table. The food was already on the table and ready to be served. *They must have been ready to eat when I arrived*, I thought. The food was probably fairly cold by now.

"Jenny," I said turning to look at her. "You'd better get these kids fed. I know they've waited long enough already. And … I'm going to get out of here and leave you alone. But I'll tell you what I want you to do. Tomorrow morning I'm sending someone over to pick you up, to take you to the school to register Johnny. I'm going to call the welfare department and tell them that Jimmy Joe has left and deserted you with these kids, so that they will help you out until you can find other means, such as a job or something. The main thing though … promise me you will never tell that story again … you know, the one about the circles of blue … to nobody! They may not be as understanding as I am. Ok? Will you promise me that?"

A smile spread across Jenny's face. She knew I wasn't going to turn her in for what she had done. "I promise!" she said happily. "Oh I sure do promise, I'll never mention it again as long as I live! Thank you so much for giving me another chance!" She threw her arms around me giving me a tight hug.

"Hey you just take care of those kids ok?" I said pulling free from her grasp. "And remember what I said about the story. Not a word! Ok?"

"Oh I'll remember. I sure will!" she said as she pulled away and looked at her kids sitting around the table. "Hey would you like to stay and eat? I'm really a pretty fair cook."

I looked at the nice spread on the table decked with corn on the cob, greens, and freshly baked bread. In the center of the array was a large delicious looking pork roast smothered in roasted apples. A cold chill ran down my spine, as I pictured Jimmy Joe. I shivered as I looked back at Jenny and smiled. "No," I said, "I think I'll pass this time. But thanks anyways for asking."

The Lamp

He walked slowly, looking at the vacant stretch of highway that lay before him. The vaporizing heat from the cooked pavement was burning its way through the worn rubber of the soles of his shoes. He cupped his hand over his sweaty brow, shading his eyes as he looked toward the sun, in an effort to see at what point in the sky it was located. He could tell by its position that it was getting close to three in the afternoon. It had been nearly two hours since the last car had passed him by, unconcerned of his baking body. He stepped off the hot pavement hoping to find some relief for his hot, tired feet in the sand. He noticed the dried splinters of grass sticking through the pavement, knowing how hard they must have struggled having to force their way through the cracks, only to die from the heat of an unyielding sun and the lack of water.

Beside a thick clump of dried grass, the sparkle of a reflected shiny object caught his eye. A quick examination from him showed it to be a can, which had probably been heaved carelessly by a passing motorist. He prodded the can gently with his toe, walking it with ease down the edge of the highway. He played it back and forth between the insides of his shoes, then kicking it slightly ahead so he could see if he was faster by running and jumping in front of it—in order to stop it before it stopped itself. He tired quickly of the sport and gave his new found companion one last swift kick, sending it scurrying across the pavement to the other side. It stopped abruptly as it made contact with something hidden in the brush, making a clanging sound like metal hitting metal. Curiously, he crossed the road and pushed the brush aside to see what it was that his can had discovered.

Protruding from the sandy dirt under the brush, he could see a shiny pointed object. Reaching down, he grabbed the object and wrestled it free from its partial grave. Holding it up, he admired his new find. This was much better than the can, he thought, looking it over as he wiped some of the dirt from its surface. Yes … this was much better.

The object was strange, like something he had never seen. It was short and long like a narrowed teapot. *What was it?* he wondered, turning it in his hands; it strongly resembled a lamp—a lamp such as one he remembered from children's books, which housed a genie, who would gladly appear to whomever would rub the lamp, and grant them three wishes. He looked at the lamp wondering if such a genie would appear for him, should he rub its side. *Should I?* he thought. He looked around, feeling foolish as if someone was watching him, knowing for certain there was no one around for miles. *Maybe I shouldn't rush this*, he thought. *What if it did work and the genie would want me to choose my choices quickly? Yeah ... I need time to think about this*. He squatted by the side of the road, holding the lamp out in front of him between his bent knees, turning it over slowly in his hands, looking at it, studying it.

What would it be—money, a new house, a new car, a beautiful woman that would love only him and him alone? Or maybe he could wish for retribution for callous deeds done against him by some estranged enemy. What would it be? What did he want more than anything else in the world? He knew that most would wish for money. That would seem to be the most logical wish, but would it be right for him? Could money be the answer to all his problems, when it never was before? He knew about money, yes he knew all too well about money.

He had struggled by working hard and using keen maneuvering techniques, in order to accumulate the things that most people regarded as success. He had a nice home, one which any man would have been proud of; a home he could feel relaxed in and comforted by. He had a good job, which he had worked hard to acquire by slowly working his way up the ladder to the position he had instilled in his mind when first coming to the company. He was proud of his accomplishments as any man would have been, knowing that the results of what he had achieved were the products of only *his* wit and capabilities.

He had a family—a wife and son, which at one time was the absolute center of his life and to what he contributed his success. His only wish at that time was to provide them with the kind of life he had never had.

An attempt to make a good life better led him into a compulsive gambling habit. He had always gambled; gambling was his only vise. He had always used the reasoning that life itself was a gamble. As his gambling increased so did his gambling debts. The more he made, the more he chose to throw away. He found himself in constant arguments with his wife, which only gave him extra excuses to stay away from home, and continue his futile attempt at one good win; however, when he did win, he would just up his ante, losing not only his winnings but much, much more. His losing led to his drinking; his life became meaningless; he stayed in a drunken stupor most of the time, and his judgment became poor, both at gambling and at work. The company finally had to let him go because of his unreliability. His final fatality finally hit, when he returned home one night in his usual drunken state, and after hearing the same lecture he had heard several times before about how he was throwing away his life and everything he cared about, something inside him snapped.

"How do you know what I want?" His words slurring as he stood weaving before his wife. "You!? You think it's *you* I wanted?" His voice raged with contempt and sarcasm. "Well don't think too hard, because *you're* not the one I wanted. You're just the one I got—the one I ended up with, because the one I wanted didn't want me—plain and simple, now you know." He threw his arms in the air, wildly laughing, then sat down and placed his head in his hands. He looked at her. The expression on her face quickly brought him to his senses. He could feel the life being drawn from him. The alcohol had made him disclose the one secret he had promised himself never to do. He knew it was too late now to recant the brutal slurs he had slammed at his unsuspecting victim.

A few days later he returned home to find the house vacant. Everything was gone, picked clean right down to the bare dusty floors—everything, including his wife and son. He had tried desperately to make amends for his actions, and had promised never to touch the poison again, but could feel the distance between them; he knew things would never be the same. He noticed an opened letter lying on the bare floor, and he snatched it up. It was a foreclosure; now everything was gone and he had only himself to blame.

He looked at the lamp he was holding. No, happiness didn't come in the shape of dollar signs, that much he knew. All he owned now was the small sack of his belongings which he carried on his back. He had never been as content with life as he presently was, with nothing to show but life itself.

What then would he wish for, if not money? What? What would someone else wish for? Revenge? Maybe for an unforeseen tragedy to befall his worse enemy? Only, now that he had nothing, he also had no enemies.

He could, however, remember a time he would have wished for revenge—one day when he was at the beach with his family trying to relax, when a known enemy of his had riled him to a point of anger he had never before reached. At this point he had silently wished something terrible to happen to this person so he wouldn't have to face him again. Shortly afterwards, he caught sight of him in deep water being sucked under by a wave. Frantically he dove into the water and swam swiftly in order to save the life of the same person he had only moments before wished death upon. The thoughts of his carelessly bestowed wish didn't return until he was on top of the man, praying and working relentlessly in order to restore his wished away life. It was when the man finally gurgled and gasped for breath, that he realized how stupid the wish had been. Never again would he wish such a thing on another person.

He twisted the lamp around looking at the other side. *Not money, not revenge*, he thought, *what about love?* Yes, he could wish for love. He rubbed his head in thought as he held the lamp out in front of him. He wondered if love would be the right thing. How should he word it? He knew that even love had no guarantees.

He had been in love before, but the two times he had fallen head over heels in love, it was with others who didn't feel the same toward him. So if he was to wish for love, who could say that she would love him? And to wish for someone to love him could be an even greater tragedy because maybe he wouldn't love her. It was confusing; love had always been confusing to him.

After his true love had run off and married an almost complete stranger, someone she had only known a few days—he quickly rebounded in order to keep his feelings hid, and married the girl his mother had wanted him to marry. He thought that in time he would grow to love her, which he did, but was never *in* love with her, which was a major error he didn't anticipate until he met the second love of his life. This woman he would have gladly given up anything and everything for; he found out though when he finally built up enough nerve to display his feelings for her, that she didn't feel the same. He continued with his farce of a marriage for years, until his wife left him after he poured out his heart in a drunken outburst.

So should he wish for love or not? It would surely be a wasted wish. Besides who in their right mind would want a love knowing it came only through the power of a genie.

He looked at the sun. It had moved further across the sky. He knew it was getting late and if he didn't get a move on, he was going to be stranded at night in the desert. As he stood up, he looked at the lamp he held in his hand.

Enough of this game, he thought. This was something he didn't need right now, extra baggage. Just something more to add to the load he had to carry. "I don't need you," he whispered, slapping the side of the lamp with his free hand, brushing some of the caked dirt from its surface and exposing a part of its shiny body. "What I need is a ride." He ran down the deserted highway, drew back and heaved the lamp high in the air, shouting, "a ride! All I need is a ride!" The lamp soared through the air catching the radiating glare of the sun, reflecting a bright blue circular glow before making a flat sounding thud as it touched down in the sandy dirt. He stood watching it as it fell and came to its final rest, then turned and walked away, kicking his feet across the pavement as he strolled back across the street.

He thought he heard the faint purr of an engine running. *The sun is starting to play tricks*, he thought, turning to look in the direction of the sound. In the distance he could see a car racing rapidly toward him. As it got closer he saw it was a bright red Sedan, and it slowed as it neared him. It pulled to a stop beside him and he lowered his head to see through the partially opened side glass. Inside was a young woman seated behind the wheel, her blonde hair swayed gently from the soft breeze blowing through the opened window. She turned toward him smiling at his bent form positioned against her car and the awe-stricken amazed expression that filled every line in his face, as he stared in disbelief at this mirage beauty of the desert. His thoughts about the lamp (that he had so inconceivably thrown away) came racing back to his mind to stagger his very existence—as she whispered in a beguiling, charming voice, "I believe you were wanting a ride?"

The Guardian

It had been a terrible day. I was glad that the workday had finally come to a close; nothing had gone the way it was supposed to go. It was a typical Murphy's Law day. I stood at the corner waiting to cross, sucking in the warm fresh breeze, as if the air itself would wipe the day out of my weighted thoughts. I crossed the street trailing behind the group of working people that had gathered at the crossing. I felt someone from behind push me, just as I heard the screeching brakes from a truck. I went sailing across the crosswalk and into the backs of the people who had just crossed in front of me. I picked myself up and looked at the large box truck that had stopped, covering the crosswalk. *I would have gotten hit*, I thought, as I tried to see who it was on the other side of the truck who had saved me from certain injury or even death—but I could see no one.

"Are you alright?" One of the women I had fallen into asked me as she helped to brush me off.

"Yes," I replied. "Did you see who it was that pushed me?"

"Pushed you?" she asked inquisitively. "Nobody pushed you. I looked around as soon as I heard the brakes squeal. I saw you jump from the path of that truck. There was no one behind you. You were the only one in the crosswalk at that time."

I looked at her knowing I had a puzzled look on my face. *I know someone pushed me. I could still feel the strong force of their hands touching my back. She must be so upset over the incident that she didn't notice.* I thanked the crowd for their concern and for helping me up, and headed on my way home.

I needed to get things ready for a camping trip the next day that I really wasn't looking forward to, and this little episode with the truck hadn't helped to ease my mind any. That and the way the day had went at work, made me believe I was on a streak of misfortune.

I turned onto the street I lived on which looked nearly deserted. I usually wasn't this late getting home and the street was usually filled with people when I walked it. *Oh well*, I thought, *it's only two blocks to my apartment, and at least it's still daylight.* As I passed the entrance of a shaded alley, my heart dropped as a hand reached out of the shadows and grabbed my arm, pulling me into the darkened area. "Got any money, woman?" The man whispered in a hoarse, demanding voice, as he pushed me against the rough, brick wall. I could see another man standing behind him and I felt my heart pounding as I feared for my life. Suddenly there was a loud racket sounding like metal trash cans being thrown around, coming from farther down the alley. Both men looked in the direction of the noise. "Hey! What do you guys think you're doing?" The powerful voice bellowed out echoing against the decaying walls. Both of the men backed away from me and tore out of the alley running off in the direction I had come. I leaned back into the wall dreading what might be coming out of the alley, but didn't have the ability to move my legs. I waited but the noise had stopped; only total silence prevailed. I took a deep breath, regained my instinct to escape this horror I was facing, and forced everything in me to start running. I ran the other block and a half to my building, and waited until I was safe inside my apartment before I breathed a sigh of relief. Two close calls in one day. I was certain now that I was surely on an unlucky path.

I woke the next morning still tired from a restless sleep. I had had awful nightmares about the man in the alley. In my dreams I saw him. As he walked from the depths of the darkened alley toward me, I could clearly see him: a tall black man with penetrating blue eyes. As he came toward me, he held his hands out in front of him as if he was ready to grab me, then he suddenly faded from my view.

Strange dream, I thought, as I hurriedly grabbed a cup of coffee. It was time for my friends to pick me up. Oh, how I wanted to cancel this whole trip. I would have, gladly, if it hadn't been for promising them, and for the fact that we had talked about these plans now for two months. I knew they would never forgive me if I backed out now. I had backed out of previously planned trips before and had promised faithfully I wouldn't this time. *Well*, I thought, trying to humor myself, *maybe this is just what I need, to get away from the rat race for a while.* I failed immensely at convincing myself though, because I had no want whatsoever for this trip. I couldn't even imagine how they had been able to have talked me into it.

I pulled my camping gear out from the back of my friend's van. I hadn't been to this park since I was a kid; I wasn't much of a camper, and an unhappy one at that. After we set up camp and fixed a small quick lunch, we decided to take a walk down the trail—this I didn't mind; I liked walking where I considered it to be safe territory. *Wouldn't find many muggers out here*, I thought, as we walked down the trail looking at the spring blossoms of the wild flowers that lined the pathway. As we crossed a small stream with wild ducks swimming, I felt some of the heaviness being lifted from my mind. *Maybe this is what I needed*, I thought, *just to get away from it all. I was already starting to feel like a new person. This wasn't so bad. No, I rather liked it.* I felt something hard in my boot. *I must have picked up a stone*, I thought, as I sat down on a log to remove my boot. "You guys go on" I yelled at my friends who were already quite a ways ahead of me. "I won't be long; I've got something in my boot." They motioned to me as one of them hollered back "don't be too long. A bear will get you." They were both laughing as they walked off. I cleared my boot and started back down the trail toward them. I came to an area that forked in two directions. I wondered which trail to take and decided on taking the one to the right, thinking it should lead me back to the campsite. I had gone quite a ways when I came to a clearing overlooking a beautiful view—it was overwhelmingly breathtaking. I walked out on the ledge of a large rock and stood, sucking in the beautiful sight of the towering mountains before me, shadowing the deep ravine below me. Suddenly, I felt the rock cracking and splitting beneath my feet. I felt myself sinking inches and knew I was about to fall to my death. I felt arms wrapping themselves around me as the rock crumbled away from under my feet, suspending me in mid air. Suddenly, I was caught up in a sweet scent which carried me to a memory of the past. It was an aroma that I had experienced before, but not for a long time. I felt myself floating in time.

I saw myself swimming in a lake; I was young and had gone out too far; I was too tired to make the swim back to shore. I felt myself going under and I knew I couldn't make it. My body slid beneath the surface of the waves, and then was jerked back by a strong arm that encircled my chest. The sweet smell of the person's body engulfed me as he swam back to shore with my limp body pulled closely to his. I was so groggy with the despairing endeavor and the brief encounter with death that I couldn't quite make out the figure of the man who had so miraculously saved me, but the scent of his body remained embedded in my memory.

I looked down at the strong arms that held me as my feet dangled above the empty space that had previously been the rock I had been standing on, and allowed the sweet scent to allure me to another period of time in my hidden memory.

I saw myself walking in the park in the middle of the day with a friend. I was about twelve years old at the time. We saw a string of outside lights lying on the ground, and I picked up the end of the wire. It looked like it had been cut. I stood looking around for the other section, and spotted it hidden in the tall grass. I reached down and grabbed the loose wire. Suddenly I went sailing through the air as two hundred and twenty volts of electricity went racing through my body. The wire was gripped in my hand and I couldn't release it, having no control over my unresponsive muscles. I felt someone's arms reach around me, pulling me away from the clutches of the electrical monster. I picked my shaking body up out of the disheveled pile which I had become. I could still smell the scent of the stranger who had saved me. I looked at my friend. "Who grabbed me?" I asked. "Grabbed you?" She questioned. "No one grabbed you. You just pulled away from the wire." I was too tired to argue the point, but the person's smell was carried to my memory to await another encounter.

I felt the arms that were holding me pull me back away from the ledge where I had been standing admiring the lovely view. I held tightly to the arms, not wanting to let them go. I wanted to see who carried the smell of my past memories. I held fast until my feet were once again stable on the firm ground. I turned to face my Savior, the one whose essence had only lingered from the scents implanted in my memories. I looked into the eyes of the angel who had saved me from certain death. I looked into the dark face of the black man who stood before me. His hair was long and shaggy, his clothes ragged and dirty. The deep penetrating blue eyes seemed to smile at me from the angelic calmness of his face. "Who are you?" I asked, still trying to catch my breath from the most terrifying peril I had ever encountered. "You don't know?" He answered with a question as his accented broken dialect rang through my ears. "I am the Guardian—your guardian, to be exact, and I must say you have kept me busy the past few days. Do try to be more careful in the future. Please?" I stood staring at him, not believing what I was seeing as he faded into nothing.

"Hey! Are you alright?" I looked and saw my friends come running toward me. Allie ran up and gave me a powerful hug. "Oh my god! I saw you standing on that ledge when it gave way. We were down below. I thought for sure you were a goner. I still can't imagine how you managed to jump that far." I looked at her grief-stricken face. There was no need to try to explain things. "Not to worry," I said calmly, looking at her as I tried to force my shaking body to laugh in order to make her feel better. "My guardian angel was here."

Dream House

The house stood back away from the road, upon the terraced lot, pitched against the blue-gray sky, which gave it a bold but lonely appearance as it faced the wrath of the wind—beating against its paint-peeled naked structure. Loose boards from the porch's ceiling waved as the wind picked up its fury again causing them to dance in the cool March air. Although the sun was bright, the temperature gave no notice, causing Cassie to pull her coat tightly against her neck, warding off the bite of the bitter breeze. Spring wasn't far off and she knew that this would be the right time to buy a house that needed as much work as this one did. She stood gazing at the unkempt house with its missing shutters and ragged appearance. This was the house of her dreams, the one she had always wanted. She recalled standing in the same spot as a child, longing to see the inside. She had often stood in front of it and stared curiously at the old woman sitting in the upstairs window peering at her through the sheer curtains. She had always been drawn to this house—as if the house itself was calling to her—it had been her lifetime dream to have the opportunity to own it. She looked up at the window she had stared at so many times before. The reflecting sun sent blue beams of circled light causing her to shade her eyes from it. There was something strange about this house, something she couldn't quite put her finger on, but she knew she was ready for whatever it had in store for her, and soon she would be seeing the inside of the house of her dreams, for the first time. She was ecstatic!

She heard a car pull to a stop. She turned to look, and saw it was Kate, the realtor, the person she had been waiting on. Now her heart was beating faster. She knew she was within minutes of walking into her dream. She was within a heartbeat of seeing whatever it was she had craved for so long.

The creaking of the front door startled her as Kate pushed it opened, causing her to jump. "Guess that thing hasn't been opened for a while!" She said laughing. "Looks like it could use a little oil, for sure!"

The inside looked almost as forlorn as the outside had. As Cassie entered the house, she was overcome by the musty smell of the closed-up inhabited house, which seemed to suck the breath from her lungs. Directly across from the entry door was a large red brick fireplace that had several bricks missing, and others that were chipped and broken. The walls had faded wallpaper left from some forgotten age; some pieces had peeled from the dampness of the house, which caused them to hang in a limp fashion. Sections of the wall were bare where the wallpaper had removed itself, entirely exposing cracked plaster with splintering laths showing through. There were boxes of old dust-covered newspapers and magazines setting around on the floor in a disheveled array.

Cassie followed Kate through a doorway leading to a room to their left, which had a double stairway and a padlocked door that was beside the first staircase. To the right was a wide open doorway, which led them to a rather grotesque kitchen area. The bare floors had some of the boards missing; there was a built in counter with a deep washtub-like sink. A hand pump was to the left, bolted to the counter with its spigot directly over the sink. There were no cabinets, but instead a pantry located across from the counter with its door hanging by one bent hinge.

Kate walked back through the door they had entered from and headed toward the staircase closest to the wall. "Come on," she said, as she proceeded to climb the stairs with Cassie trailing after her, "I'll show you the bedrooms." Cassie held tightly to the dusty banister, not noticing the elegance of the wood, or the craftsmanship, but being thankful for the stability of its firmness, fearing that the creaking, cracked steps may at any time give way.

Directly across from the top of the stairs was a room with a door standing open. Kate walked into the room with Cassie following closely behind. The room was small with maybe just enough room for a small bed and dresser. The walls were in a lot better shape than the ones she had seen in the kitchen and living room. She wondered if they would be good under the wallpaper that was covering them, or if they would come apart in pieces when the paper was removed.

Back in the hall, they went across to a door that was on the left side of the stairs and opened it. Cassie got a cold chill as Kate flung the door open. This room was in the worst shape; it looked as though someone had already stripped the wall paper. The walls were bare and the plaster was cracked in places, but not as bad as the living room had been. The floor was very rough, however, it had a large hole in the middle of the room. *Strange*, Cassie thought as she walked around the hole and looked in, seeing the laths with plaster protruding through the gaps for the ceiling down below them.

One door remained down the hall in the opposite direction from which they had come; it was the bedroom that faced the front of the house; the one she had stared at so many times as a child. Kate started to open the door and found it was stuck. She pushed against it with some force, sending it flying open. Again, the forced stale air was overpowering, leaving Cassie breathless and gasping for air. She could feel a presence in the room causing pictures to flash through her mind. She walked over to the window, which still had the dirty shear curtains hanging from it, and looked out. She could see the hazy figure of a child standing below on the sidewalk. Her vision wasn't clear at first, being obscured by the thick drifting fog like substance that seemed to appear from out of nowhere. Then the fog seemed to lift and she could see who the child was—it was her! She was standing, looking up as she had done so many times in the past. Suddenly, she felt closeness to the old woman as if she was seeing through her eyes. This old woman, who the whole neighborhood had ridiculed and spoke of as if she was some demon from hell, waiting to cast an evil spell on whomever should stray into her territory, wasn't the wicked creature she had been taken for. This woman had wanted so much to speak to the child who stood on her sidewalk and stared at her. She wondered why this child didn't run away with the others who stood calling her names and throwing things at her house. She had longed for a child of her own, but was childless due to a boating accident that had taken away the one love of her life, leaving her bitter against the world, and causing her to stay secluded from others—hiding away in her lonely house until she died from her broken heart.

Cassie jerked herself away from the window shaking her head, trying to clear her jumbled thoughts. *God, what was that?!* She thought to herself. Why was she suddenly seeing visions? She looked around the bedroom; this indeed was the master bedroom. On one wall was a beautiful fireplace with the wood around it brilliantly carved. A lavishly decked chandelier hung from the center of the room. This was the first thing that she had seen in this house that was of any value. She couldn't imagine why it hadn't been removed. "I wonder why that is still there." She said to Kate, pointing at the fixture.

"Who knows?" Kate replied as she stood shivering. "Have you seen enough? I am ready to get out of this room. I can't imagine why it is so cold in here; it's like we woke the dead or something."

Cassie eyed the door at the bottom of the stairs. "I suppose you want to see the basement too?" Kate said, in a voice filled with sarcasm.

"Well … yes, actually I would." Cassie replied.

The steps of thick, hand cut planks made very little sound as they slowly descended them. The musky smell was much stronger as it lingered in the dampness of the spacious basement. A few feet from the bottom of the steps sat a massive round coal furnace, which took up a large area of the basement. The walls were a mix of stone and dirty, brown brick. Fruit jars decked the shelves that lined the top section of the walls. Along the edge of the floor were more jars, some scattered and broken. Cassie walked around the furnace inspecting the condition of the walls. One wall, which was mainly brown brick, had a section of a different shade of brown about the size of a door laid horizontally. *Hmmm*, Cassie thought to herself, wondering if maybe a small root cellar wasn't sealed in. She ran her hand along the bricks feeling the difference of the texture.

Suddenly, the light in the basement grew dimmer, the haziness she had experienced earlier had returned. The pungent stench grew stronger as she felt herself being swept away into a dreamlike trance. She knew she was still in the basement, but although there was a foggy haze, the appearance of the basement seemed to be in a much newer condition. She heard the distant cry of a whimpering child. She saw him standing by the wall that she had just been looking at. *Where did he come from?* she wondered to herself. *Why was he crying? Was he hurt? He must have wandered in from the street.* She tried to get closer but she couldn't seem to move. She felt as if she was frozen; her whole body was numb and lifeless. She had no control or power over herself other than to stand and watch the child crying. The haze lightened some, and she could see the child clearer now. She could see his small, black face, although it was partially hidden behind his outstretched arms. He held his hands outward, his palms facing out flat as if to protect himself from something. Then she could see the blood running freely down his face. Suddenly, the shape of a man appeared from out of nowhere; she saw the man had a heavy stick in this hand. He raised the stick bringing it down across the boy's head. She could feel the blood running down her face and her head was pounding with pain, a pain she had never before experienced. She knew she was seeing through the eyes of the boy. She knew she *was* that boy. She screamed violently at the man to stop, but no sound was heard, except for the yelling coming from the man as he relentlessly beat the boy with the club. She watched as the boy fell to the floor in a lifeless pile. The man reached down and lifted the boy's head back, checking for signs of life—then pitched it forward causing a dead thud as it hit hard against the dirt floor. *Dirt?* she thought. *What had happened to the concrete floor? And where had this man come from?* And why was she so helpless to move when she wanted so desperately to help this child? She watched as the man took a shovel and started digging out the side of the wall. After the hole was large enough, he lifted the lifeless body and crammed him into the tight fitting hole, then shoveled the dirt back into place. He then started sealing the area with bricks. He walked past her to a small hand pump in the corner to get water to mix the mortar. She tried to reach out to grab him but she still had no control, as though she wasn't even there.

The room brightened. "Are you alright?" Kate was squatting beside her holding her head as she gently patted her face.

"What Happened?" Cassie asked, finally hearing the sound of her puzzled voice as it echoed against the bricks.

"You passed out. Don't know why or what happened. One minute you were standing here talking, and the next minute you were on the floor." She helped Cassie to her feet.

Cassie looked at the wall with the different shade of brown bricks and grabbed Kate by the arm. "Let's get the Hell out of here!"

The next morning Cassie's mother stopped in for coffee as was her normal routine. "Well," she asked as she poured her coffee. "What did you think about the house?"

"You don't even want to know, Mom," Cassie said as she set her coffee cup down on the table and reached for the box of donuts that were sitting there.

Her mother walked over to the table, and pulling out a chair sat down as she sipped the hot coffee she held in her hand. "Well, you can tell me about your dream house, but first I've got to tell you about this strange dream I had last night—before I forget what I remember!" She said excitedly, chuckling silently to herself about what she had just said. "Yes, it was a weird dream, like none I have dreamed before, that's for sure!" She took another drink of her coffee and sat it down, getting ready to tell her story. "Well I can't remember the whole dream but I sure remember the bad parts of it," she continued. "It seems like I was this boy's master or something—anyway, I beat the kid to death and buried him in a wall in a basement. I mean is that sick or what!? I would never do anything like that! I can't believe I could even dream something like that!" Cassie stared at her mother in disbelief—she couldn't believe what she had just told her. Was it a dream or a vision from the past? Could it be that her mother could have been her master in another life and had taken her life without a second thought about it? This was almost too much to comprehend. She couldn't imagine her mother as someone as mean and ruthless as that man beating the child had been. She shivered thinking about it. She picked up her coffee and took a drink as her mother asked, "so you going to tell me about the house?"

She quickly sat the cup back down and looked at her mother. "Nothing to tell," she said, her unreserved voice had a frank matter of fact tone. "I think I'm going to leave this one alone."

Trucking

The mud oozed around the soles of my shoes, their sucking pressure causing it to be more difficult to walk. My feet were becoming weighted by the packed mud that covered them. The mist of rain had soaked my hair, as I trudged the short trip across the cemetery grounds toward my car. *What a day for a funeral?* I thought. Then realizing my thoughts … *How silly of me. Really! After all, what day is a good day for a funeral?* I walked with my head down trying to shield the rain from my face. From the corner of my eye, I caught a glance of a figure of a man behind a tree, partially hidden from my view. Even through the rain, I could see that it was Don Sheets! *The nerve of him,* I thought, *showing up here. The man must truly be a vulture, waiting to pluck the pieces of flesh from her body.* He saw me notice him and quickly turned and walked in the opposite direction. I couldn't understand how some people could take advantage of someone who couldn't fend for themselves.

I reached my car and got in, shaking the water from my hair. It really hadn't been much of a funeral, only four people including the preacher. I guess Elsie Brunner wasn't the best liked person around. No, she wasn't liked by many at all; she was a hard woman to get to know.

I had met her a few years before. I was doing odd jobs at the time and had gone to her house to do some painting. We had become friends after a while, and I would often stop by to see if she needed anything. Sometimes we would sit and talk for hours, her having so much to say and no one to talk to. It was during these chats that she told me the story of her neighbor, Don Sheets.

He seemed to be such a helpful man when he had first moved into the house next to her. He was always stopping over to see if she needed anything. At the time, she was able to get around a little without constant help. He would run errands for her whenever she needed him to, and was always bringing her over a plate of food his wife had prepared. He was always the perfect gentleman, a shear pleasure to bestow, with his comforting smile and his soft soothing voice. He was always there to help do small repairs for her, just trying to save her a few bucks, as he would say. Indeed, in time, a man like that would capture anyone's heart. He never wanted pay for any services, and when offered, he would simply say, "what are friends for?" This went on for a total of four months.

He came in one day with a worried look on his face that she immediately detected. After she picked at him a while, she was able to pry from him the problem that was causing his worry. It seemed that he was trying to buy a truck, actually a semi tractor. It had always been his dream to be an independent trucker, only his loan had fallen through. He said he didn't have enough collateral; his house wasn't enough to back the loan by itself, since he had just bought it and still owed a mint on it. She suggested that maybe she could co-sign the loan for him. He told her that with this type of loan, he couldn't have a co-signer. It had to be backed with collateral from his property. Then he told her there was one way that the bank would approve it: if she could sign her house over to him long enough for him to get the loan, then he could sign it right back to her—that way he would have enough property to back him for the loan. She told him that she would have to think about it. He told her that was alright, that he would understand her not wanting to do it—after all she hardly knew him, and he doubted if he would do that for someone he knew, let alone a total stranger. A stranger, no, she didn't see him as a stranger, although she had known him only a few months. She felt very close to him and wanted to help him in his plight. He had only shown her kindness and now it was an opportunity for her to repay that kindness; she saw nothing wrong with helping out a trusting friend. "Ok," she told him, "let me know what you need for me to do or sign." He informed her that he would have his lawyer take care of everything and would bring the papers needed for her to sign. A few days later he had come back with his lawyer and two others as witnesses for the deed signing, since she wasn't able to go to the lawyer's office to sign the papers. She gladly signed the deed, without hesitation. Once alone with her, he informed her that as soon as his loan went through, he would be back with his lawyer to put the deed back into her name.

A month went by before she heard anything more from Don. It was as if he had disappeared completely. She figured he was busy with taking care of the loan and trying to get his truck, which is why she was so shocked when she received the eviction papers that were delivered to her door by a court official. She immediately called her lawyer. She explained to him what had taken place and how her neighbor had so easily persuaded her into signing her property over to him. He asked her why he hadn't been called at that time; she said she had trusted Don and his lawyer, and she didn't think anyone could be that nice and yet so deceitful at the same time. He said he would take the matter to court, and for her to not say anything to anyone about it.

In the court hearing, her lawyer tried to plea with the court how her neighbor, whom she had thought to be a good friend, had coerced her into signing the property over by trickery—that she was the victim here, not Mr. Sheets!—that he was an underhanded con-artist exploiting old ladies, and should be dealt with as such. Her lawyer didn't take long pleading her case, and she could certainly tell by the look in his face that all was lost when Don's lawyer started talking.

"Mr. Sheets here," he had said addressing the court, "had only acted in the best interest of his neighbor and friend. She had signed the said property over to him because of all the past work that he had performed for her. After all, he had done all the work on the property now for months. He has ran various errands for her and made sure that she received proper meals, and care. He has worked also by helping her to get her into bed and out. She lived alone with no proper care other than Mr. Sheets. Now, she signed the property over with the thought in mind that Mr. Sheets would continue his care of her, which is exactly what he has had in mind. Knowing that he would be on the road and not there to care for her, he thought it best that she was not in the house by herself, and knowing how stubborn she could be, thought that by evicting her she would have no other choice than go to the right facility, where she would also receive the proper treatment and care. Your Honor, a woman her age and in her health does not need to be alone."

After the statements were read by both parties, the judge came to the agreement of saying that the property would remain as it was. He said he truly felt that Mr. Sheets had acted solely for the best of his neighbor's behalf, and that he thought the property should go to Mr. Sheets after the death of the said client, because of his hard work and care in providing for her. But she could also stay in the house until her death, as long as she had proper help; he suggested that she hire herself a live- in nurse. So the property was to remain in her possession until her death—when it would be under the ownership of Don Sheets. So be it.

Don kept his distance from Elsie after that; he knew with her poor and fading health, it was only a matter of time before he would get the house, anyway—besides, with his new truck he was always on the road away from home.

Elsie had hired a nurse to stay with her and the two seemed to really hit it off. As the months passed, they became very close friends and companions, so much more than that of simply a nurse and patient relationship. It was really through Rosie, her nurse, how I came to meet the two of them. It seemed she was sick of the color of her room and wanted something brighter. She had seen my advertisement in the paper and had called me, not wanting to have any man around. I had made sure I advertised it that way, knowing that a lot of women didn't trust men. I thought it would get me some quick jobs, and I was sure right about that. I got more than I could almost handle, but by spacing my time properly, I managed to handle them all. After finishing with the room, Elsie and Rosie managed to keep me around, by always finding something that needed my attention, since I also had done minor household repairs along with some plumbing. They managed to keep me pretty active; they would also talk me into running short errands which started cutting into my work time, so I started stopping by on my off days just to talk or see if they needed anything.

Elsie was a real talker. Once you would get her talking about something, it took a lot to shut her up. She was always talking about her past; she told me several stories about when she was a young girl, about how she met her husband, and how he had died. Her favorite story though was about how her neighbor had thought he had tricked her out of her house. I had heard this story several times from her, also from others. I knew that the story was about Don Sheets, and I knew him to be a very cold and calculating character whom very few trusted. She always ended the story with the remark, "he'll never get my house!" Her voice always seemed so cold and penetrating; it caused chills down my spine. Each time I had heard her say this, I thought the same thing: *he already has the house. It's only a matter of time before he can take possession of it.* I knew her failing health wouldn't allow her to be around much longer. Still, when she would make that statement, she sounded so sure and exact—I would almost believe her.

I had stopped by her house that fatal Friday, passing the ambulance as it was leaving. I found Rosie in the house alone crying; she told me that Elsie was dead before they had arrived. She was worried, not knowing what she was going to do now, and having no where to go, since she had no living relatives or friends. I told her not to worry, that she could stay at my place until she was able to find something.

The funeral had been short. The church she had left her possessions to hadn't hesitated in trying to speed up the process of getting her things auctioned off. The sale was to be a week from Friday, exactly two weeks from her death. They were already at the house going through things. I had dropped by to pick up some tools I had left there, and if it hadn't been for them being clearly marked, they would have gotten sold with Elsie's things. The church officials who were at the house when I stopped didn't want me taking anything from the house at first, until I showed them an identification and showed them the tools were clearly marked with my name and social security number.

Well, that would be sure to please Don; I knew this way he, too, would get the house a lot faster. I wondered why he had bothered coming to the cemetery though. I looked back at the tree where I had seen him standing. There was no sign of him anywhere. It was raining harder now. *He has probably left,* I thought, *hmmm ... maybe he thought he could also get the gold out of her teeth.* I thought of Elsie, and her saying, *he'll never get this house.* "Sorry, Elsie," I said aloud, "but it looks like you were wrong."

A few days later, I returned home after completing a small job, and for some reason I felt completely drained. Guess the week's happenings had finally taken its toll on me. I decided to lie down and take a nap before worrying about what I was going to fix for supper. I'd drifted off to a sound sleep, and started dreaming ...

I saw Don Sheets pulling into a tire store with his new truck; he told the man to replace the front tires. Shortly afterwards, he pulled the truck back onto the highway, and was driving along a mountain road. The scenery was lovely. The sun was out and it was a beautiful day. Then suddenly there was a passenger in the seat beside him. It was Elsie! He thought he had seen someone out of the corner of his eye and glanced at the passenger seat briefly, then shot his head back quickly, gawking at the passenger who had appeared from nowhere. "No!" He shouted. "You're not here! You! You're dead!" She sat staring at him and his shocked, dumbfounded gaze with his eyes protruding, and she smiled with a devilish, impish smile, and said nothing. Suddenly, a loud explosion sounded, his front tire had blown. Don gripped the steering wheel tightly trying to regain control of the truck as it swerved to the other side of the road, then back again. He could hear Elsie laughing deliriously as the truck plunged itself down a steep embankment, flopping as it went, and rolling end over end until it came to an abrupt stop by smacking into a tree; it immediately burst into flames. Don was pinned in, the steering wheel wrapped tightly against his chest. He tried to push with all he was worth to move the steering wheel, but it wouldn't budge. He could see Elsie still smiling at him through the smokey cab. Then she suddenly faded as the flames of the burning truck engulfed his screaming body. He allowed one final scream to escape him before sliding into unconsciousness.

I awoke in a sweat. *What a dream ... terrible! Guess I just had too much on my mind.* I went in the kitchen to find something to fix for supper.

The next morning after I got my cup of coffee and opened the paper to see what kind of world I would be facing today, my coffee cup slipped from my hands as the shocking headline caught my eye: **Local Man Killed in Fiery Freak Truck Accident!**

Once In a Lifetime

From my rear view mirror, I watched the dark clouds of dust being kicked into swirling circles from the tires of my car. The unkempt road obviously wasn't traveled on by very many, for it had shoots of grass growing through the cracks of the asphalt. I drove with care, trying to miss the uncountable number of spots of missing pavement. The bright, Virginia sun blasted its powerful rays of light through my windshield. Even with sunglasses on, the haloed blue circles dancing on the glass made if difficult to see, causing me to pull the visor down to keep them shaded from my eyes.

I was on my way to meet a friend, whom I had never met in person. Anticipation filled me as I wondered about this first meeting. I was always apprehensive meeting people for the first time. Would she be the same fun-loving person that she portrayed herself to be? Would she be the same laid back, caring and considerate person I had talked to on-line every day for months? I found it was much easier to tell a total stranger things you wouldn't normally tell those with whom you were more acquainted with. Therefore, she knew more about me than anyone else knew, and I had never even seen a picture of her or spoke with her on the phone. Although I had met with others I had talked to on-line before, we had never really discussed meeting in person, until my job decided to send me to a seminar in a town in Virginia that was only about thirty miles from where she lived. She seemed a little despondent when I first mentioned it to her, but said it was only because she felt she needed to get her house in shape. I told her it really wasn't necessary to worry about such trivial things. I wanted to meet *her*, not her house. After we talked about it, she was obviously more relaxed about the matter, and then we both looked forward to our first meeting.

I hit a large pot hole in the road, which jilted me back to reality. The road had gotten a lot rougher and made me wonder how long it had been in such desperate need of repair. I saw another road up ahead of me to the right, and slowed down so I could read the road sign. *Chapels Road*, this was the road I was looking for. I turned right onto a much nicer road. *This is better*, I thought, *maybe I can make better time now.*

I started thinking about the strange circumstances which had caused us to meet in the first place. On that particular day, I had gotten home from work, tired and cranky and in no real mood for any company, other than my on-line friends who usually help me unwind. My boss had been on my back for the biggest part of the day; I wondered how much longer I would be able to take his harassment, before moving on to another job that might be a little more serene.

I poured myself a cup of coffee, kicked off my shoes, and headed for the living room to my computer, hoping to find some of my on-line friends to talk to. I sipped my coffee as I checked out my list to see who was on line. I noticed a name on my list that hadn't been there before. *Where did that come from?* I thought. "That's strange," I said out loud to myself. "Where did you come from?" I knew I hadn't put this name on my list. *Who are you?* I wondered as I checked out the profile for the screen name, *LivinisGr8*. The profile gave me no clues as to who this person was. *Well*, I thought, *I'll just instant message her and find out*. I sent an I M wondering if she would respond. "Hi," I wrote, and she responded back with a, "hi … how r u?" I returned with a, "who are you??" Her comeback was, "a friend." We continued talking, and I found it to be a very relaxing conversation. She seemed to know me right from the beginning. I thought that maybe it was an older friend I hadn't spoken with in months, and maybe I had just forgotten the name. It wasn't likely though, I very rarely, if at all, forgot names.

I had been going on line now for the past year and had met a lot of interesting people. I had even met some of them in person and had enjoyed their company over dinner, playing golf, or for an active evening at parties, or cook outs. Yes, the computer had opened up a new window in my life. It had given me the opportunity to meet with people I would have never otherwise met. With my constant struggle at work, I needed people I could relax with, and wasn't one to feel right about going places alone to try and meet others. I enjoyed the chat rooms. You get to know and feel at ease with people you talk to every day. Of course there were a few strange ones, but that was to be expected.

Over the next few months, we talked nearly every day on the computer. We had become very close friends, and got along very well. We had only exchanged the basic facts about ourselves at first, but over the months we got to know a lot of personal things about each other.

Her name was Angela, but she went by Angel. She lived on the outskirts of a small town in Virginia. She had lived there all her life, only leaving for the years it took her to finish college, then returning to the same house; this was the house she was born in, and she said she was content enough to live out her entire life there. Her parents had died in a car wreck while she was in college, leaving her the house and their belongings, and she couldn't bring herself to part with even one item. After college, she had started a small business from which she was able to make a decent living.

When I got the news about my company sending me to a seminar, I was ecstatic—we would finally be able to meet in person. Angel didn't seem to be as excited about it as I was, though. *Maybe she doesn't want to meet me*, I thought. There had been a lot of paranoia caused from on-line meetings going bad. I asked her if that was the problem. "Oh no," she said. "It's just that I was thinking I need to get the house in shape for your visit. I would love to meet you, by all means."

Over the next month before the seminar, we talked about our upcoming meeting and how great it was going to be. The closer it got to the day, the more excited we became. Now the day was finally here.

I saw the number on the faded mailbox and turned into the lane heading toward the house. The small, yellow house nestled in the midst of a shallow grove of leafy red maples was very welcoming to the eye. Its homey appearance made me feel at ease when I walked up the few steps leading to the door; the door opened quickly before I got a chance to knock. In the doorway stood a tall blond woman smiling at me; although I knew she was forty seven, her youthful appearance portrayed her to be in her mid or late twenties. Before any words were spoken, she hurried out to greet me with an affectionate hug.

"Oh Barb," she said excitedly as her words bubbled out with a tinge of a southern accent. "I never thought you would get here. I'm so glad to finally meet you in person."

"I'm glad too," I said, still holding on to my newly met friend, whom I had talked to for so many months. I could feel the bond between us, knowing neither wanted to let go.

"Come on in," she said as she broke loose from the embrace and grabbed onto my hand, directing me into the house. "I've got lunch fixed. We'll eat first, then I'll show you around the place and we'll talk, only this time in person instead of on line. LOL?" The computer jargon she used for laughing out loud, which she had suddenly used for everyday talk, caused us both to burst into laughter. After a good home cooked meal, like one I hadn't had in quite a while, we idled the day away talking about our wants and wishes, and different computer friends and happenings. Later in the afternoon she started prompting me about my leaving, saying I needed to leave soon or I would get caught in the dark on these roads.

"Gee," I said laughingly, "you'd think you were trying to get rid of me or something."

"No, not at all, it's just that I don't want you to get caught on these back roads in the dark, especially the rough one."

"Oh, I'm just joking." I said, trying to laugh off the stupid statement I had made. "But you are right; I wouldn't want to be on that road in the dark. Guess I had better be going."

We said our goodbyes and I drove down the driveway and onto the road, having the dreaded feeling of leaving my friend behind, but being thankful for the closeness we had encountered over the last few hours. We had gone from great on-line acquaintances to having a very close, personal friendship. We had bonded over the past hours into an amity I knew would last a lifetime.

As I started to pull onto the rough road, I remembered that I had left behind the drawings and pictures she had given me. *I haven't gone so far that I couldn't go back and get them*, I thought, as I turned the car around and headed back in the direction from which I had come. I slowed as I neared the driveway; I stopped the car and sat looking at what I thought had been the same place I had left only minutes earlier. The mailbox was gone and the post was decayed and falling apart; the lane was overgrown in weeds and brush. In the midst of a few parched and deadened trees, stood the fallen remains of a burned down dwelling, with its blackened, charred boards reaching upward out of the heavy growth of ivy covering it, and exposing the only evidence that any house ever existed there. *This can't be the same place*, I thought, as I looked around at other familiar markings which led me to believe that this had to be the right area. I was absorbed in thought about what was taking place. *Did I only dream I was here? How could a place disappear in only a matter of minutes? Was I losing my mind?* I got back in my car and turned around, heading away from this phenomenon I had encountered.

It was almost dark when I stopped to get gas at the small station at the edge of town. "Could I ask you something?" I asked the older man behind the counter as he took the money I was handing him to pay for the gas I had pumped.

"Sure," he replied. "What's up?"

I was just wondering if you knew anyone by the name of Collins around here?" I asked waiting for my change from the twenty I had given him.

"Hmmm," he mumbled. "Yeah, I know a Sam Collins. He lives in town." He reached over the counter and handed me my change.

"How about an Angela Collins, do you know her?" I asked inquisitively.

"No, can't say that I do," he answered. I turned and started to leave as he hollered at me. "Wait a minute," he said. "I remember a family that used to live outside of town, about twelve miles out, by the name of Collins. I'm sure they had a daughter by the name of Angel or something like that."

"Well do you know where they are now?" I asked looking back at the man as he rubbed his chin, with a pondering look on his face.

"Sure do," he replied. "They're dead."

"Oh, you mean her *parents* are. Yes I know. Car wreck, wasn't it?"

He looked at me with a distant stare to his eyes. "No, it wasn't a wreck, it was a fire. And it wasn't just her parents either. It was all three of them. As I recall, about twenty years ago there was a bad fire. Old Jacobs Road outside of town was in bad need of repair at that time. The fire truck wrecked when it hit a large pot hole, rolled and injured three firemen; they never made it to the fire. The house burned down, and Andy Collins, his wife, and their daughter, Angel were all killed in that fire."

I couldn't believe what I was hearing. *Who had I met? Did I dream this whole thing up? Was I hallucinating?* I was standing beside the door when the old man walked over to me. "Sure glad they got that road fixed," he said. "Sometimes it takes something terrible to happen to wake *some* people up. They have never let it get in that shape again though. Why you asking, anyways? Do you want to buy their place or something? I don't think it's for sale, though. The town has left it that way as a reminder of what tax dollars do for this town. That way when someone starts complaining, they tell them to take a run out there and see what can happen when proper repairs aren't made on the roads."

I looked at him and shook my head. "No," I said as I headed out the door. "Just someone I once knew."

I walked outside and breathed in the night air; I took a deep breath and tried to clear my head. I felt dumbfounded, not wanting to believe the ordeal that I had been through. I stepped down from the walkway onto the pavement and headed for my car, still shaking my head in disbelief. I heard the phone in the booth at the corner of the building start to ring. I stopped in my tracks and turned to look at it—no one was around. I had always had a terrible compulsion to answer a ringing phone. I stood looking at the phone that was still endlessly ringing, and giving in to my urges to answer it, rushed over and grabbed it up off its hook. "Hello?" I said, responsively into the phone, as I waited for some reply from a stranger.

"Barb? Barb is that you?" The voice echoed through my body, shocking my entire being.

"Angel?" I answered in disbelief. "Angel, how in the world!? What is going on here!? Where are you!?" The words all seemed to run together, I was astounded, I couldn't believe this was happening. "Where are you?" I repeated, somewhat firmer now, starting to get upset thinking this was just a poor excuse for a bad joke. Then into my ear her softly spoken words flowed.

"Where else?" she whispered, laughingly. "I'm on the Internet, of course!"

The Breaking Point

I woke suddenly with a jerk. It was still dark, not quite time to get up yet.
I lay staring into the darkness of the room—not total darkness, mind you, for
it was accompanied by a small light coming from another room, which was
left on to help control the darkness; I was not one who enjoyed being in the
dark. I had tried sleeping once in an entirely solid dark room; it really hadn't
mattered that it was a large room, because being in a coffin couldn't have
been much different. That was when I first discovered my claustrophobia.

I had awoke through the night and was overwhelmed by the complete
absence of light; the emptiness I felt was like being sealed in a box. Not being
able to sense the size of the space I was in caused me to feel smothered. I
started gasping for air, but the air seemed to evade me. I knew I needed to
open a door, but where was it? I couldn't move. It was as though I was being
held down by some unknown force. I felt myself being tossed into a total state
of nonexistence, being swept away into a black hole of space. My senses
started to fade into a blank nothingness. Suddenly, the door opened and the
light infiltrated the room, bringing me back to reality. My cat had pushed the
door opened and saved me from my chaotic endeavor. After that, I always
made sure I had some light in the room and a flashlight on the night stand
beside my bed.

I lay there in the semi dark room thinking about the dream I had been
dreaming. In my dream, there was an enormous white building faced with tall
marble pillars. The large, double doors were always chained and padlocked.
I would walk around the building looking for a way in, but could never find
one. I had dreamed about this place so many times that I was familiar with
every part of the outside. What was this dream telling me? Why could I never

get inside? Was there something I was trying to find or was there something I needed to avoid? The dream had me puzzled.

I had dreamed the same dream several times before. I was always very young in the dream, maybe fourteen or fifteen years old; those had been my most troubled years—as with most people.

As a teen, I was always in trouble of some sort. My parents were constantly fighting, and when they weren't fighting, they were drunk. I alienated myself from them as much as I could. I was always gone. I stayed away whenever it was possible, running the streets or staying with friends. I hated my life, but I hated my parents more. I hated being with them, and always being the butt end of their stupid jokes, or having to clean up after them whenever they would have their drunken parties. I made a promise to myself at that point in my life that I would most certainly not follow in their footsteps. It was funny remembering back because I had dreamed about the strange building at that time also; once, the chains had been hanging freely until I got close to them, then they locked themselves quickly, barring the doors from me once again.

The dream remained on my mind the biggest part of the day. *Why did I keep thinking about it*? I wondered. *Was I getting closer to finding a way to get inside the sealed structure? Did I really want to get inside?* It seemed that I always had the dream during certain stages in my life when I felt my life was in turmoil.

I had been going through a heartfelt romantic endeavor now for close to two months. It had actually been the best time of my life, but I was now also facing the worst. We had been split up for nearly a week, and it was starting to get the best of me. It seemed there was no possible way we could get along. We were constantly fighting, always over some meaningless idiotic subject, and there were a lot of times we would forget what the subject even was. Whenever we were together, is seemed that no two people were meant for each other more than we were. *So then why all the constant fighting*? I knew that a lot of the fighting stemmed from my jealousy. I knew I needed to do something about my jealousy, but what? It seemed to be something which I had no real control over. Why was I constantly working myself up into a total upheaval over nothing? Yes, it was nothing, I knew that, a casual glance at some passer by, or a polite, kind greeting or word when meeting someone would all but send me into a silent rage, only to be dealt with later as an open, verbal, heated confrontation. *Where was this leading me?* I knew I needed desperately to change my way of thinking, either that or I would be heading down a long, lonely road.

The evening treated me to a quick TV dinner, which I ate alone while watching the news. *The whole world seems to be going crazy,* I thought, as I listened about another school shooting, and about a mother who had beat her small daughter to death with the cast on her arm. There was also a story about the brutal treatment of a pony that was locked away for years in a stall, causing its hooves to grow to an outrageous length; and because of the scarcity of food, it had eaten away at the wood from the boards on the stall. *People can be so cruel.* I decided I had seen enough television for one night, and figured a nice relaxing walk would be more sufficient before bedtime came.

Later, I lay awake in bed thinking of the coming day. I had been offered a new position with the company I was with, and had been weighing the possibilities of this placing for a week now. I had to give them my decision tomorrow and still wasn't sure of what it should be. I knew the job would definitely give me more money and more prestige with the company—it would also take me away from the people I had become friends with over the years, and enjoyed working with. I would also be losing some of my free time, being required to spend more hours at work, and being a part of higher management. I knew the work I would be doing would also add a lot to my stress level, as if I didn't already have enough. It was a hard decision for anyone to make, but I was fairly certain I would take the job; after all, it wasn't every day that a person got the opportunity to climb the ladder of success. I closed my eyes and drifted off into a troublesome sleep ...

I was in a dense fog. In the distance, I could see a dim light shining through the hazy mist. As I got closer I saw it was a stupendous white stone building with four gigantic marble pillars facing the front. I saw a large doorway housing two immense wooden oak doors. A heavy, linked chain was running through the handles of the doors and padlocked link to link, binding them together to avoid entry into the building. The building looked familiar. Maybe I had seen it once in a dream; I stood looking at the doors wondering if perhaps there wasn't another way in. Suddenly, the chains broke away and hung loosely through the handle of one of the doors—I couldn't believe it. I stood staring at the chain, still swinging from the weight of falling free; I was amazed at what had just occurred. I pulled the heavy door open, and shivered as it creaked with age, having been sealed for so long. Inside was a dimly lit passageway. I could see more light coming from the end of the seemingly long corridor, and decided to see what it led to. At the end of the corridor was a doorway where the diverging white light was projecting itself from. I walked into the light and felt a strange aura surrounding me as the light penetrated my skin.

I squinted trying to see past the haze that seemed to engulf the lighted area. I kept slowly walking, hoping to find a way through the cloudiness. Finally, I could make out some figures in the distance. As I got closer, I walked out of the mist, and was able to clearly see and hear the people in the distance standing beside an opened area.

A man stood staring at me and motioned for me to come to him. As I got closer to the man, I noticed that the opened area was actually a swimming pool filled with people laughing and having fun. The man looked out of place though, since he was dressed in a nice three piece, dark suit. As I walked up to him, he smiled at me and waved his hand motioning toward the pool. "See all the people enjoying themselves?" He asked.

"Yes I do," I answered, still wondering about his appearance.

"These are the ones that made the right choices in life" he said, continuing. "You see, everyone has choices. We all have paths to follow. Each path is a new journey. However, sometimes we will choose the wrong paths, which can lead to heartache and chaos. These people, here, chose the right path and their lives and the people around them are better off because of the choices they made. Because they made the right choices, their lives are now easier and they are reaping the benefits of having found the right way. They are rejoicing, having made the right decisions. They have put the concerns of others before petty selfishness; they contemplated a long-term prospect and weathered the storm to find their serenity, rather than a brief encounter with a short-term, happy triumph that usually goes sour in time. They were definitely not the ones to *chuck it all* for the thrill of the moment. No, they considered the outcome before they went along with their final decision, or in other words, chose to take the right path. There are, of course, the thrill seekers, those that are willing to sacrifice their whole future on a whim or an idea—although sometimes these are the right choices, if they put no one at stake other then themselves.

"Could giving up a job you like for a better paying one, be one of these wrong paths that people might take?" I asked, thinking about the job I had to make a decision on.

"Oh yes," he said, "as a matter of fact, most that choose the wrong paths are for those reasons exactly—choosing a job for money or prestige, thinking they are getting ahead, when they are actually only digging themselves in a hole. Or an unsecured love affair, because of the hurry up attitude they seem to have instead of waiting for the right one to come along. These things will usually take some people right over the edge, where they can end up in a suicide or homicide situation—this is known as the breaking point.

I looked at the people swimming and having fun. "So, if these are the ones that took the right path, where are the ones that didn't?" I asked as I turned and looked at the suited man again.

He pointed toward the end of the pool. "See that hedge at the end of the pool?" He asked calmly, his eyes appearing void of any emotion. I looked at the tall, thickly grown hedge that was growing across the end of the lengthy pool. "Well," he said, "they're on the other side."

"They're on the other side?" I said, repeating his statement as a question. "What are they doing on the other side?" I figured the pool extended beyond the hedges.

"Come with me," he said, motioning for me to follow him as he headed toward the area of the hedges. As I walked around the end of the hedges, I noticed the pool did indeed extend to the other side as well.

"So," I said to the man, "then you're telling me that if you take the wrong path, you end up the same as you do taking the right one?"

"Not at all," he said. "Walk closer and see for yourself." As I got closer to the side of the pool, I could see the people that were jumping in were bloody and bruised. The closer I got, I could see why: the pool had no water in it. They were throwing themselves into an empty pool, only to be bashed against the rough concrete bottom.

"Oh, my God," I exclaimed as I looked into the pool lined with broken, bloody bodies. "Why are they doing that!?"

"Whenever a person takes the wrong path, they are forever beating themselves to pieces as they struggle through each torturous day of their despicable life, forever regretting the move that they made." He put his hand on my shoulder. "We not only hurt ourselves in the process," he continued, "but others as well, and sometimes may cause them to also take wrong paths throughout their lives."

"So how do we know the correct path to choose?" I asked as I looked into his hardened, black, staring eyes. "Just how are we supposed to know beforehand?"

"Instinct," he said. "If you just follow your heart and keep the thought of others in your mind, you should do all right."

I awoke the next morning feeling rather enlightened, and then recalling the dream I had had, my body shivered. My mind raced through the ordeals I had been encountering over the past month: my break up with the love of my life and my unexpected promotion. *Could these two things or one of them be what the dream was all about? Was I about to take the wrong path in my life and not be able to turn back?* I was told by the man in my dream to follow my heart, and that was as good advice as any. I decided to call Terry that evening to talk about our situation, and try to reconcile our relationship. I knew I would have to curtail some of my jealousy, which I would promise to do. I guess it was a start, and I had to start somewhere if I was going to follow what was in my heart.

I went immediately to my boss's office as soon as I got to work. "Mr. Stafford," I said, addressing him as I entered the room. "I need to talk to you about the promotion."

"Sure, sure," he said pointing toward a chair. "Grab a seat."

"No," I said, "that's quite all right. This won't take long. The thing is, I'm turning down the promotion."

"You're what?" he said with a look of astonishment on his face. "Are you telling me you don't want to get ahead in this company?"

"No sir, that's not what I'm saying." I spoke calmly, so calm that even *I* was amazed. "What I'm saying is that sometimes there are more important issues than simply getting ahead. One thing that is more important than merely getting ahead is being satisfied, and I'm very satisfied with what I do. I really don't feel that I'm ready for a change at this time. For me to change right now may not be the best thing for the company. Satisfaction makes for better productivity. I know there are several people that want this position, and would probably be better at it than what I would be presently. Maybe later down the road I'll be ready for a change, but my gut feeling is to stay put at this time, I feel I need to follow my heart."

I left his office and headed back to mine and my regular job; I felt good about the decision I had made. Sure, I had turned down the promotion, knowing that it would have been more money and more prestige, but I knew it wouldn't have benefitted me to have made that kind of change as of yet. I had followed my heart, and I was sure I had taken the right path. My boss had admired me for standing my ground because he also felt I would be more beneficial to the company in my present position—he had showed his appreciation by giving me a nice raise.

Now I knew I needed to get things right with Terry. I was anxious to try to restore our relationship and I knew that we needed to sit down and have a long talk, just the two of us. I headed down the hallway toward the elevator. I couldn't wait to get in my office and give Terry a call.

I thought of the dream and of the man with the three piece suit. Now I understood what he was showing me; now I knew the secret to the building that I had sought all my life—the building that had evaded me in my past had now opened itself to me—the building that had haunted my dreams for so long was in actuality, my inner self, telling me to find the right path by following my heart. From now on, I would do just that!

As I neared the elevator, I saw a man in a nice suit standing, staring at me. He smiled and nodded; I smiled back at him in acknowledgment, then quickly turned away to avoid his gaze. I thought I had seen this man before but couldn't remember where. I slowed my pace not wanting to get on the same elevator that he was getting on. As the elevator door was closing, I caught another quick glimpse of his face and his strange emotionless eyes, and it hit me ... he was the man from my dream!

End of the Line

The reflection of the headlights from an oncoming car caused a hypnotizing effect. The light kept dancing through the down-pouring rain as it beat against her windshield, creating little explosions of light through the rhythm of the wipers, and playing tricks on her weary mind. She knew she was exhausted. She knew she needed to stop soon and get some rest. She had been on the road now for nearly six hours without stopping and it was becoming harder for her to concentrate on her driving. Her mind kept drifting back, hashing over the events that had taken place that day. She couldn't believe the way things had happened, which had led her to where she was now, driving in this down pour and fighting against her exhausted body's urge to sleep. Had she really followed through on her mindless endeavors? Had she really done the unbelievable task which had inhabited her daily thoughts? Had she really killed her husband?

She had been through some very trying times. Sometimes she had felt as if she would completely lose her mind. Her marriage had been a downfall almost from the beginning, but of course it hadn't started out like that. *Oh, how easily we are deceived ...* she thought, trying to recall the rest of the saying, but it failed to come to mind.

The rain continued beating against her windshield. The wipers were no longer much help, and she could hardly make out the tail lights of the car ahead of her. She knew she needed to find a place to stop, but she kept driving in the down-pouring rain as her mind kept recalling past events.

She had met Ross in high school. He had caught her eye the first time they had passed each other in the hallway. He was the new boy in school, and was very good looking. At lunchtime during his first week, he had managed to find a seat available beside her in the cafeteria—*she* had also caught *his* eye. They started talking and he finally got the courage to ask her out.

He was courteous and considerate on a date, always asking her what she would like to do. Almost from the beginning, she knew that he was the one she wanted to marry and spend an eternity with. They planned on getting married right after they finished college—they both went to local colleges so they could still see each other and be able to save money in order to fulfill their plans.

They had a small wedding with just a few friends present. They wanted everything to go right, and it did, at least for a while ...

At first, Ross had been very attentive and seemed so caring toward her that she felt she had truly married an angel instead of a man. After a few months, the bills started mounting because Ross thought there was no end to the spending, and always wanted things they just couldn't afford. He developed a short temper, and would flare up over nothing. She thought that with her going to work, a lot of the pressure would be lightened and his temper would go back to normal, but things got worse. Along with raging over the bills, he also became overly jealous and started accusing her of having someone on the side whom she was secretly seeing.

Then an unforeseen pregnancy threw their plans into turmoil. Pressure seemed to build as the pregnancy caused additional problems. The doctor bills grew and although her pregnancy was almost full term, the baby was stillborn. Her hopes of the baby being a calming effect for Ross died along with her dreams in that hospital. After that, he started drinking more. Then one night he had come home drunk as usual, she tried talking reasonably to him trying to make him see what he was doing to their marriage, when suddenly he went into a maniacal rage and started hitting her. The next morning, he was overly sympathetic and so sorry over the ordeal, swearing it would never happen again. Things went smoothly for a few months, but then he flared up again, this time over an incident at work. However, this time he never showed any remorse. The beatings continued whenever he would have too much to drink or was just in a bad mood.

A car in front of her tapped its brakes, shaking her back to reality. *Where had that car come from? The tail lights seemed to have appeared from nowhere.* She knew she needed to get off this highway and get some rest; she had been driving for too long, much too long. She wondered how long it had actually been since she had made her escape from her beaten-down, abused way of life. How long had she been driving? Six hours? Seven hours? And where was she headed? She had no idea. She was just putting space between her and her past. She had tried leaving Ross before, but he always managed to find her and bring her back, then the abuse was only worse. Once, when she had moved back in with her mother, he told her if *that* happened again, he would hurt her mother worse than he had hurt her. "You're mine," he would say, "and don't you ever forget it!" That was the last attempt at leaving him. She knew there was only one solution: she had to kill him. He was the one who had driven her to this low point in her life. This was her last resort, her only way out.

The rain beat steadily against the windshield. She was having a difficult time watching the car ahead of her, which kept tapping its brakes. She knew that the people in front of her were probably having trouble seeing the road in all this rain, also. Suddenly, the car tapped again, then quickly veered off to the right, exiting the freeway. *Damn*, she thought, another exit and she missed it again. How long would she have to go before she would find another exit on this hell bent highway?

The freeway now seemed vacant except for her. Her mind started drifting again, recapping the events of that day. She had always thought of various ways of doing away with her husband, whenever he would come in drinking and slapping her around, but she never really thought she'd actually carry it out. That day had started out like many others. He had gotten up with a hangover from being out the night before drinking with his buddies. When she set his breakfast in front of him, he immediately swept it off the table and onto the floor. "You know that's not how I like my eggs, you bitch!" He shouted as he sent his coffee cup sailing through the air, hitting hard, splattering against the wall, close to her head. "Who the hell wants coffee without breakfast?" He grunted as he jumped up from the table knocking his chair over as he rose. "I'm out of here," he hollered as he headed toward the front door. "I'm going to find me some decent breakfast." She stood there silently staring at the mess he had made. She knew she needed to get it up before he returned or she would feel his wrath even worse than before.

Her friends, the few friends she had left, always asked her why she took so much abuse, but she had no answer for them; although she had tried to hide the abuse from them, they had finally seen through her masquerade. She knew there were only two ways out of a situation like this, suicide or homicide. She cleaned the mess, then waited for him to return. When he didn't return home by five that evening, she went ahead and started supper, knowing it had to be on the table by six thirty, if he should happen to be home by then, or she would have hell to pay. It was seven o'clock when he finally came in; he had been drinking again. She figured he would start in on her about supper being cold, but instead he sat quietly and ate. His silence, however, was short-lived. He kept watching her as he wolfed down his food, like a man who hadn't seen a meal in a long time. He stopped eating and sat staring at her with gravy drooling down his chin. "You know," he said, slurring his words—"if you weren't so frail and ugly, I might stay home more, but as it is, the only thing you got going for you is your cooking, and then you got the nerve to serve it cold." With that, he picked up the plate and flung it toward her, striking her arm. She backed up against the sink, looking at him through fearful eyes, anticipating his next move. "What're you lookin' at, Bitch?" he shouted. "Not my fault you can't even get your cooking right. I should teach you a lesson about how to treat your man." He jumped up from the table, and grabbed her by the arm he had just struck with the plate. She cringed in pain, pulling away from his grip. Quickly his hand flew across her face, backhanding her and causing her to fall against the sink, hitting her back on the edge of the counter. He walked over toward her with his fists raised. "Oh what's the use?" he said, shaking his head. "I'm really not in the mood for this tonight, I'm going to bed. You clean this mess up. I'll take care of you in the morning, Bitch!" She didn't even notice him when he left the kitchen. She just stood looking at the mess knowing she should get busy and clean it up, but what he had said was still ringing in her ears. He was going to take care of her in the morning. She knew what that meant. She wasn't going through this again, and she knew what she had to do. She walked into the living room, and lit all the candles she had sitting around. She went back in the kitchen, and turned the gas on the kitchen stove, making sure that the pilot light wasn't lit. She looked around the kitchen as if to say a final goodbye, then grabbed her jacket off the back of the chair, and walked out the door into the adjoining garage. Under a cabinet in the garage she pulled out a small bag that had a few clothes she had hidden for such an occasion—this had been planned for a long time; she just never thought she would ever have the nerve to carry it out. It was fear that gave her the nerve. She started to get in the car but realized that she didn't have her car keys. *I put them in the kitchen drawer*, she thought. She knew she still had time. She just hated going back in, still afraid of getting caught by her husband. She rushed back in hoping the door wouldn't wake him up.

The exit sign aroused her from her thoughts of the day's happenings. *Great,* she thought, *finally an exit*. She was sure to find some sort of motel and get some much needed rest—she pulled slowly off the exit ramp. The rain hadn't slowed any and made it even harder to see on this stretch of road. The freeway was hard enough to see, but had newer paint than *this* road did, plus it had those reflectors that divided the lanes. She would just drive to the town that was coming up. She couldn't make out the town's name but she made out the miles—two miles, the sign had said. The scenery sure looked familiar, what she could see of it. If she didn't know better she would have thought it was her own town. When she came to a sharp curve in the road, she thought it was the same type of curve that was on her street. *So I guess the houses will all look like the one's on my street too*, she thought as she went around the curve. When she pulled out of the curve, she couldn't believe her eyes; it was her street. There was her house, still burning. The lights from the fire trucks lit up the neighborhood, but the rain still gave it a hazy, fog-like cover. *How did this happen? Did I get turned around somehow in the downpour?* She pulled up slowly and parked across the street from her house, and she saw an ambulance parked in front of the house too. She wondered if they had found him yet. She wanted to get out and ask them, but was afraid she would give herself away. *I could say I was visiting a friend and just got home.* Yes. That's what she would say. She had to see for herself. She had to know for sure. As she walked around the ambulance, she saw a man sitting on the curb with his head in his hands. *Could that be a firefighter who got hurt*, she wondered. (She hadn't thought about that happening.) The police were standing beside him. She saw the firemen carrying a body out. They walked it to the sidewalk behind the man, and the policeman tapped him on the shoulder. "Sir, they're ready for you to look at the body."

"Uh, ok," the man said quietly looking up. She stared at the man. She couldn't believe it. It was her husband! He was looking right at her, but it was as if he was looking through her! He didn't seem to notice her at all. Instead he got up and walked to the body on the gurney behind him. She walked closer to see who the body was, worried now that a fireman had gotten hurt. The policeman unzipped the bag revealing the body inside. She couldn't believe what she saw—when her husband saw the body he started crying. "I know I never treated her like I should have," he sobbed. "If I had been here ... if I hadn't been drinking ... if I hadn't had to go out after cigarettes, I would have been here, and probably would have been asleep. But when I opened that door last night when I got back from getting cigarettes, it just blew. I don't know what could have happened."

"Looks like those cigarettes might have saved your life, buddy," the policeman said, patting him on the back.

She looked at the body on the gurney. She couldn't believe it—it was her! She was dead! Now it was clear to her. Her husband had gone out without her knowing it. When she had gone back in the house to get her keys, he had opened the door to come in at the same time, sucking the gas quickly into the living room, causing it to blow. She never made it out of that kitchen. She had only caused *her own* death. He had only gotten tossed around a little. She had planned *his* death, but had only caused her own. Well, at least one thing was for sure, he was now a threat to her … no longer.

The Light

I woke suddenly drenched in sweat, my throat parched from the heat. Dying for a drink, I dragged my tired, limp body from the bed, and made my way to the kitchen. My legs felt as if they were weighted. The faster I tried to move, seemed only to slow me down more. *What is wrong with me?* I thought, as I inched my way down the hallway, through the living room, to the kitchen. *Maybe I am coming down with the flu? That could be the reason I am so thirsty. Maybe I am dehydrated. Maybe I am ...*

I stopped in the doorway of the kitchen, staring ahead at the wall directly opposite me. Something wasn't right. *Could I still be sleeping? Was I still dreaming?* On the wall was a large picture window, one which covered the majority of the wall. *I have to be sleeping*, I thought. *There is no way that window is really there.*

I gazed through the imaginary window; it was light, very light outside. Daytime? No. I knew it was only two a.m.; it couldn't possibly be daylight yet—but it was. I saw the sun shining, glistening off leaves of the perfectly formed trees. I could see in the distance, hills—lovely, green hills. A small brook rippled its way through the grassy fields, glorified with the staggering, wild flowers that were everywhere. The green was enhanced, as an immense, vividness of illusive green deepening in its effect, causing it to be so alluring. The beautiful array was captivating to my weary eyes. The sight indeed was breathless to behold. *This isn't real*, I thought. *The green is too rich, too strong to be real, more like something you would see in a painting, or even a movie.* I stood staring at the wonderment of it all, totally amazed by the marvel I was beholding.

From the corner of my eye something distracted my view. Water was dripping from the ceiling to the left of me. I tried to see the spot it was coming from, but it seemed to appear from no certain place. The water started dripping more rapidly. *That's strange,* I thought, wondering where it was coming from. The sun was shining, and the ceiling leaking. Leaking? Well, there really wasn't any evidence of a leak. I remembered that my stepfather had seen water dripping from the ceiling shortly before he died. The thought made me shiver; *am I dying,* I wondered, *or dreaming?* Something wasn't right.

I looked down—I was standing on a lighted disc. There was a pale blue light circling my bare feet. The light was winding around my feet in a counter clockwise movement. Slowly, it proceeded to rise from the floor, circling still as it made its way progressively up, past my ankles, then higher, enclosing my legs in its radiant light. The light found its way up, abducting my whole body inside its captivating exuberance. I could feel the tiredness and pain being lifted from my aching body. It felt good. I felt great! I had never felt so free; free from any thoughts of aches or pain. I felt like a different person entirely. *Was this really happening?* I stood still, not wanting to move one part of myself from the cylinder that engulfed my new body, my painless body. I felt the cylinder being lifted into the air. Something told me to stay inside the cylinder of light. I was careful not to allow any part of my body to escape the warm healing serenity of the divine light. Thoughts of the green visionary fields that I had viewed through the window reflected on my imaginative mentality. *What was happening? Was this a dream? Where was this cylinder taking me?* The cylinder sailed smoothly, gliding easily through the air. Through the living room and down the hall it traveled carrying me, its only passenger, with care. Slowly, with caution it moved, allowing time to study everything we passed. As we entered the bedroom, I noticed two people lying in the bed. Drawing closer I could see that I was lying in the bed next to my husband; I wasn't moving, I knew I was dead. The cylinder was heading more rapidly now for the wall facing my side of the bed. In that instant, I knew if I went through that wall I would be gone, vanished, into another dimension. *No, I couldn't die!* I didn't want my husband to wake up and find me dead in the bed beside him. I threw my arms out of the cylinder to stop myself from going through the wall. "Oh God … no!" I screamed, holding my arms out with palms flat to protect me from penetrating the wall. Everything faded, I was in total darkness. I could hear someone talking off in the distance. The sound was coming closer; I felt someone shaking me by the shoulder. "Hey, are you going to sleep all day?" It was my husband. I had been dreaming.

I poured myself a cup of coffee while staring at the wall, which I had seen the picture window in. *What a strange dream,* I thought. *Wonder why I would dream something like that?* I walked over to the table and sat down, with my imaginary world still lingering in my mind, and joined my husband, who was reading the morning paper. "Anything interesting?" I asked, making idle conversation. He laid the paper down and looked at me.

"Let me tell you about my dream," he said. *His dream?* I thought, *he should hear mine.* But I remained quiet and looked at him attentively ready to listen to his story. "But I really don't think I was asleep," he continued. "So I'm not sure if it was a dream or if it was real. But anyway, something woke me up last night. It felt like someone was in the house, but I couldn't get out of the bed. So I lay there staring at the doorway, wondering if someone was going to come in, then this little blue light, about the size of a dime comes floating into the room. It was moving kind of slow. Then when it got closer to the bed, it picked up speed. Then all of a sudden, it went flying right through the wall on your side of the bed. What do you think of that? Strange dream … huh?"

I set my coffee down. I was shaking too much to hold it. Questions were running through my mind. *Was it a dream? Was it pure coincidence that our dreams matched? Did it really happen?* I looked at my husband who was waiting for some remark from me about his dream. I picked my coffee up and sipped at the hot brew. "Yeah," I answered calmly, "that sure enough was a strange dream."

The Deep Sleep

The song blaring on the radio was making my head throb. I reached for the button, while keeping my eyes focused on the road, and quickly changed the station. "That's better!" I said out loud to myself. I was alone in the car, but I always had the strange habit of verbalizing my thoughts. This habit of mine became very noticeable at work, and I would always use the follow up, "as long as I didn't answer myself." Being the joker I was, I always managed to get a laugh out of that.

It had been an exceptionally long day; I had been working a lot of overtime all week, but today I stayed even longer than usual. It was starting to turn dark. I was already dead tired and had a good twenty miles yet to drive.

Today was my birthday, my fortieth. "Maybe I'm working too hard for a person my age," I said talking aloud to myself again. "Whoops there I go again." I started laughing. *If it's bad to answer yourself,* I thought, *what about when you catch yourself?*

The radio caught my attention again. This time the station had picked up some static. I reached for the button to adjust the tuning, glancing at it momentarily to direct the aim of my fingers. I focused quickly on the radio then right back at the road. From out of nowhere there suddenly appeared a shattering ray of bright light from a car's headlights, heading directly toward me. With my vision impaired by the obscuring brightness of the lights, I jerked the steering wheel sharply, trying to avoid a head on collision.

I felt myself being twisted and turned. I knew the car was rolling end over end. I felt a piercing pain in my side that seemed to radiate throughout my body. I knew that something had penetrated my right side and went through to the left. *Oh God, I'm going to die,* I thought, as different things went racing through my mind. Darkness covered me, and I thought that maybe I had been blinded by the incident. The sound of the radio and the roar of the motor running suddenly distanced itself from me, until it faded totally into silence.

My senses were aroused by the brilliance of a white light. *Maybe the other person wrecked too,* I thought, thinking the light must have been coming from the other car. The light grew brighter, engulfing me with its alluring rays, just short of blinding me. I tried squinting my eyes in order to see beyond it, but the light was too strong. I tried turning away from it but found I couldn't move. I could only close my eyes in order to avoid its penetrating brightness.

I thought about my wife waiting at home for me. *What if I die, or am I already dead? What would she do if I died?* The questions rolled through my mind. *How would she react to the call, or would they tell her in person? She never had to make any decisions by herself before. Could she handle it?* She had been acting tired lately, not really her normal cheery self. No, it was as if something was bothering her, something weighing on her mind. Was it all the overtime I had been working? She was becoming very distant to me. We never really talked anymore, but whose fault was that? It was always late when I got home and then I was so tired that I usually fell asleep on the couch watching television, where I would sleep until morning. So what could be bothering her? Why hadn't I noticed this before? Had I become so involved in getting ahead at work that I had allowed my family to become second to my job? Had I become so focused on being able to obtain a few luxury items that I had lost sight of the basics? Had I become the man my father had been? My father, who alienated himself from his family and friends, as he struggled to get ahead at his job, had caused his wife to seek affection in the arms of another, leaving behind her husband and children in exchange for a little happiness. Was my wife doing the same? Had I driven her away with my thoughtlessness? Had I been too concerned and selfish thinking of only fulfilling my own personal wants and egotistical whims, to allow the one thing that meant the most to me—my soul purpose for living, to slip away? Had I, like my father, caused my wife to seek satisfaction elsewhere? I thought about how irritable and tired she had become. Could these have been signs? Yes I knew that they could well have been, but I hadn't thought about it before. No, it had taken dying to bring me back to reality. Yes, it had taken dying to get me to see what I had missed in living, what I had allowed to fade from my life while I still had life in me. Now it was too late. Now I was gone, leaving behind the one that meant so much to me, the one I had never taken the time to show, or let know how much she really meant to me. Leaving her alone to face all the hardship and misery of burying a husband and trying to sort out and get all his affairs in order, before she could continue on with her life. Now I wished I had prepared her more. *I wish I had allowed her to be more involved in the running of everything, so she wouldn't feel so lost now.* But now, it was too late, I was dead. *Dead? Did I say dead? Was I dead? Why was I thinking this way?* I wasn't dead yet, I was still in the car, holding my eyes closed to shield them from the blinding light of the other car's headlights.

I felt a gentle touch to the back of my hand, and wondered what it could be. *Could someone or something be in the car with me?* The sensation of the touch grew stronger. *Someone is patting my hand,* I thought. Although I was curious, wondering who the person was, I kept my eyes shut tightly, not wanting to expose them to the brightness of the light again. The rubbing and patting of my hand became rougher almost like a slapping rather than a patting, arousing me, making me more aware of the distant voices that seemed to be getting closer. *What's that?* I thought. *Who are they calling to? Danka? Who is Danka? Not me. They couldn't be talking to me.* My name wasn't Danka. It was John. I could hear them again. This time it was closer and clearer. "Better put the shade over her, she's waking now." I tried to speak but my body seemed to be paralyzed.

Through the slits of my closed eyes, I could see the bright light had faded some, making it more tolerable to my sensitive eyes. I eased my eyes open cautiously, making certain the light had dimmed before fully exposing them. I realized I was in a room, a clean white room from what I could make out. I could see hazy figures standing around me, looking down at me as I lay stretched out before them. They appeared to be doctors, or some sort of emergency workers. *How did I get here? I must have passed out. Was this a hospital?* I didn't remember them transporting me to the hospital. It seemed to have been instantaneous. The last thing I remembered was the bright light and closing my eyes to shield them from it. But I never seemed to lose my sense of awareness of what was happening. Never seemed to … I must have. I must have been out for quite a while to have been transported this far. I knew the closest hospital was at least twenty miles from where I had wrecked. I looked up; there was a plastic dome covering me, shading the brightness of the light above me, as it bounced off the dome causing blue circles of light to dance above me. I tried to turn my head to see the figures of the people I was hearing around me, but still was unable to move. I could see from the corner of my eyes the one standing closest to me. My vision was clearing and I was able to focus better on the person to my left side. I could make out the smooth shiny features of the clear non-wrinkled blemish-free skin on his face. His satin white-blond hair fell softly to his shoulders. I was held spellbound by his angelic appearance. I was able to slightly turn my head and caught sight of some of the others. They all looked alike, not identical but all having the same features and same satin white-blond hair. *Who were these people?* I thought *Were they angels? Was I dead?* I tried to speak but my jaw felt like it was wired shut. *Maybe they were angels,* I thought, as I had flash backs of the accident. My eyes darted back and forth checking them out. I counted three.

"You'll be alright, Danka." One of them said as he smiled down at me through the shield. His voice was soothing, but there was that name again. Who the hell was he talking to? I wanted to scream … "I'm not Danka!" but it was useless. My lips were sealed—for the time being anyway. Maybe they had me confused with someone else. I began to feel sensations of life coming back to my body. I found myself being able to move.

I turned my head to the right and was able to see the size of the room. It was enormous. There were rows of platforms lined as far as I could see, all having the shield cover over them. Most of the beds or platforms had someone in them, but a few were vacant.

What was happening to me? Was this some sort of waiting place after you die? I tried to coax myself to believe I was in a hospital, but I couldn't make myself believe it. This was not like any hospital I had ever seen before. This was so strange; I knew I might as well face the facts; I was dead; I had to be. This place was so strange and different it must have been heaven or a waiting place before heaven.

The angelic-like man leaned over the dome and smiled at me. "I need to check you out now, Danka," he said as he opened up a small window on the side of the dome lid. He reached in and took hold of my wrist. He stuck a little suction cup to the back of my wrist that was wired to a device he held in his hand. "We need to see if you are ready to come back yet, Danka." His smile faded as he looked down at the monitored device. A puzzled look came over his face. He looked around and motioned for another one of the strange-looking creatures who seemed older than the first one. I recognized him as one that I had seen while peering out through the slits in my eyes. He held the hand device toward him as he walked over. "Would you look at this?" he said questioningly. "She doesn't seem to be ready yet. Does she?" The older man looked at the strange monitor the first man held in his hand. "Oh no," he said, "she definitely isn't ready yet." Then the man looked at me and said in a calm serene voice, "I'm sorry, Danka, but it seems we have to send you back. It seems you haven't fulfilled your journey or learned your lesson yet." I opened my mouth to speak. My voice was cracking and hoarse, but still I was able to get my words to come out. "I don't know what the hell you two are talking about!" I said. "Who are you? And what am I doing here? And who the hell is Danka? My name is John." The questions all ran together. I was getting overly agitated about the whole ordeal.

"I know this all seems a little confusing to you," the older man said. "Please let me try to explain. You were sent away because of your lack of co-operation and your inability to slow yourself down. You always were in a rush to do things. You always tried to take on more than what we saw as a reasonable workload. We don't do things like that; We needed you to see what it was like in a rushed world, and thought that the rush of things would help you to slow down and really look at the important things in life. Now it seems that the life you have been living in this rushed world hasn't helped you at all. You have allowed the fast pace to overwhelm you and have ignored the value of the things that are truly important. In that world, you have a mate that cares a lot for you, but you choose to let your work take over your life, and put her wants and needs on hold. Now she is on the verge of suicide, something your uncaring ways have caused. Before we can bring you back, you must straighten out your life there and learn what life is really all about. You need to slow down, Danka."

I thought about my wife and how she had seemed so distant—to think she had considered suicide? Oh no! What was I thinking? Why did I think that work should always come first? Why couldn't I have seen the signs? Now, was I too late to change it? "You're sending me back?" I mumbled to the older man, my voice still cracking from the numbness in my throat. "Does that mean you are sending me back to where I was ... back to my wife? I will change things if I can go back. I promise I'll change things."

"Yes Danka, we will send you back to your fast-paced world, and I hope the next time you return, things will be different. I hope that this time the lesson will be well learned. Find out what life is really about, Danka. Find out that by slowing down you can see things as they really are, and not just a blur of a world passing by. Life is very important, Danka. Cherish it while you have time."

He reached through the opening with a small pen like object and touched my arm with it. I felt my body going numb, then darkness overcame me. I could hear distant voices in the background.

"John? John, are you with us John? I think he's starting to come around, Ma'am." The voice grew stronger. "Try talking to him, Ma'am, I'm sure he can hear you now."

"John … John, can you hear me?" The voice seemed familiar. Yes! I knew that voice. It was my wife's voice. I was back! Back in my body! Back with my wife! Had it just been a dream? Maybe it was, maybe not. Who knows or cares! I was back, and that was all I cared about. I was given a second chance. Oh, thank you, God, I prayed. Thank you for allowing me to come back. Or—thank them … well whoever it was … I opened my eyes and looked at my wife. There was something different. *What is it?* I thought. Maybe it was me. Maybe I was just really looking at her for the first time—for the first time, seeing the love radiate from her eyes. How could I have been so blind in the past to not have seen how much she cared for me? I knew how much I truly cared for her now. Things were going to be different from now on.

"Hi, Honey," I said, my voice still cracking and hoarse. I felt her hand tighten around mine.

"I was so worried," she whispered as the tears that she had held back so firmly overran the brim of her eyelids and rolled down her cheeks.

"Don't worry, Honey," I whispered to her. "I know I haven't been there for you lately, always trying to make more money, and get further up the ladder. Guess it took this to shake some sense into me. You are the only thing and the only one that matters to me. Without you, I don't know what I would do. I'm so sorry, Honey, but things are going to be better, and *that* I swear to you." I saw the look that covered her face, a mixture of disbelief and relief, and I smiled at her. "Honey," I continued, "when I get out of here, I'm going to take just the two of us on a second honeymoon, only this time it's going to mean a lot more than before. It's going to be the beginning of a new life for us."

"He's going to be alright, Ma'am," the doctor standing behind my wife said as he was filling out his paperwork. He had his back toward us. He turned and smiled at me as he was leaving; his pale blond hair softly hanging to his shoulders gave his face a haloed radiance. I was awestruck! "Now you make sure you slow down a little, okay? Huh, John?"

I didn't answer. I was looking at his name tag, which had the name ... Danka!

Happy

Michael walked out the back door of his house leading to the yard. He was glad to have the work-day over and to finally be home. He had hurried home as he usually did in order to have extra time to spend with his daughter. The people at work couldn't understand the closeness he felt to his daughter, always spending his free time with her, instead of going out with friends. He saw her sitting by the fence staring at the road. This was her usual place, so she could watch the cars and see him coming home. He looked at his daughter, her little frail figure sitting in that small wheel chair. He wondered if he would ever see her run again, or even walk. It had been two years now since the accident. The doctors didn't know why she couldn't walk; they said it was nothing physical. Maybe she had a mental block caused from having her dead mother, who was flung across her in the accident, lay on top of her for a about three hours holding her down. Even though she was only four years old at the time, maybe it was the weight of her mother that was still holding her down. He had taken her to various counselors, but nothing seemed to help.

He walked over to her and reached down to give her a hug—she didn't move. She continued to stare at the road, her expression blank and sad. "What's wrong, Susan?" he asked as he brushed her tangled hair from her taunted face. "Look!" she said, pointing at the road. "Someone just hit her and left her to die."

He looked in the direction she had pointed. She had been staring at a small black and white cat. She lay on the edge of the road, her body lifeless, with the wind ruffling her matted fur. She was a pitiful sight indeed. "Yes. That's a shame," he mumbled, as he thought how some people could be so cruel to hit some poor defenseless animal, and drive off without concern of whether it was alive or dead.

"She needs buried before she gets hit again." Then in a soft breaking voice she asked, "will you bury her, Daddy?"

"I'm sure that the owner will do that as soon as he discovers that she's been hit, Susan," he said.

"But what if she doesn't have an owner? What if she's just a stray? What if the owner doesn't look for her, thinking she just ran away? What if her owner doesn't care?" All these questions were thrown too quickly for him to be able to come up with a valid reason of *why not*. He shrugged his shoulders.

"Ok, Susan," he answered. "If it will make you feel better, I'll bury her. Now *where* should we bury her?" he asked quietly, thinking out loud as he looked around.

"Let's bury her over by the shed, Daddy. That way I can watch her grave and make sure it is taken care of."

He took the wheel barrow and a shovel and went out the side gate to get the cat. He was able to find an old shoe box large enough to fit her in. After he covered the hole, he stomped the dirt down and pulled a couple of small flowers from the garden to place on her grave. Susan smiled, "I think I will call her Happy, because I know she is happier now," she said. "I can just feel it."

"Why would you want to name a dead cat, Susan?" he asked, looking at her puzzled.

"Well, we need to have a name to put on the marker for her grave, don't we? And besides everyone needs a name, don't they; if you're talking about them, how are you going to know who you are talking about, right?"

He looked at her and smiled. This little girl was so logical at times it was hard to imagine her only being six. "Well ok then, Susan, I guess your right, now I think we better go in and eat our supper. I'm sure Carol has had it on the table for quite a while now." He twisted her around quickly in her wheel chair, making her giggle, and wheeled her into the house.

After supper, Michael sat with Susan watching TV. "Daddy," she asked quietly, "will you make Happy a marker tomorrow, for her grave?" He looked at his little daughter sitting beside him on the couch. He smiled thinking how good her heart was and how she was always concerned about something other than herself. She never complained about anything to do with her ailment. She was a wonder to him.

"We'll see, Honey," he said "I should be able to make her something. I don't know how good it will look, but I will make her something. Ok?"

"Ok, Daddy," she said. "And if *you* make it, it's got to be good."

He smiled. She had a way of warming his heart. "Now I think it's time for bed, we have a lot to do tomorrow."

Susan woke suddenly, what was it that woke her? There was something sitting on her, pulling at her covers to wake her up. The house was dimly lit and smelled of smoke. She couldn't quite make out the figure on the bed with her. Then she heard a high pitch shrill of a cat. There was a cat on her bed. Where did a cat come from? The urgency of the cat's voice and the consistency of her pulling at the covers made Susan realize there was an emergency and she needed to get up.

"Daddy!" she yelled as loud as she could. "Daddy, get up! I smell smoke!" Within moments, her father came bumbling through the door.

"Oh my God," he hollered. "I've got to get you out of here, the house is on fire!" He grabbed her up in his arms and ran through the smoke filled hallway. It was hard for him to find his way through the blue circling smoke that was hanging in the air. The smoke had gotten heavier very quickly. He felt something tugging at the leg of his pajama bottoms, so he went in the direction it was pulling him. Reaching out with his free hand he found a banister at the top of the stairs. He descended the stairs slowly, watching his step. (He didn't want to fall with Susan in his arms.) He could hear the sirens of the fire trucks now outside his house, but it didn't calm the feeling of terror he felt. He knew that a lot of people had made it as far as the door in a fire and perished before opening it. He made it to the bottom of the stairs, but again found himself disoriented and wasn't sure which direction the door was. He felt the tugging once again at the leg of his pants and followed it. Suddenly, he could make out the outline of the door in front of him. He opened it and hurried out. Immediately, several firemen surrounded him; they took Susan from his grasp and rushed them both to the ambulance that had just arrived. They sat Susan on the back of the opened van and placed an oxygen mask over her mouth as they checked her for burns. They seated Michael down next to her and gave him oxygen also.

"Is anyone else in the house?" A fireman asked Michael. Michael shook his head in response to the question. Any other day, Carol, the woman that took care of Susan and the household, would have been there. But today was her day off and she had left the night before after fixing their supper, to visit with her brother.

"You sure are lucky you're a light sleeper. This was a bad one. Sure went up fast once it got started," the fireman stated. Michael removed the mask from his face. "It wasn't me," he said. "It was my daughter who woke *me*."

"So you're the hero in all this?" The fireman said, smiling at Susan. Susan pulled the mask from her face. She was watching the house, which was still in flames. "Not me," she shrilled. "It was Happy. She woke me clawing at my blanket."

"Happy? Who's Happy?" the fireman asked with a concerned look. It sounded as if a family pet had saved them, but no pet had come out of the house.

Michael looked at his daughter who was still watching the house. "No, Honey, it wasn't Happy. I'm really not sure what it was," he said, remembering the tugging at his pants leg, "but I assure you it wasn't Happy."

Again the fireman asked Michael, "sir, who is Happy? Is that your pet? If so we'll try to find him."

"No, Happy isn't our pet. She was a cat that got ran over by our house and we buried her yesterday. So I know for a fact it wasn't Happy." Michael answered.

His thoughts were interrupted by Susan's shrills. "Daddy, look! Look!" She screamed pointing up at an upstairs window. "It's Happy! She's trapped, she can't get out!"

Michael looked at the window and saw the tattered black and white cat prancing around the open, broken-glassed window. It sure looked like the cat. No, it wasn't possible!

The fireman looked at the window she had pointed to, but didn't see anything. He glanced at the other windows, but still no cat. He looked at Michael and saw the shock in his eyes as he stared at the window Susan had pointed to. What were they seeing that he couldn't see? Where was the cat? He couldn't see a cat anywhere.

Michael's mind and eyes were focused on the cat, and he didn't see his daughter push herself off the edge of the van where she was sitting, and fall onto the ground. She quickly pulled herself up and struggled slowly toward the house. Michael glanced around and saw her, but at first was too awestricken to move. He quickly revived his senses and ran to retrieve his daughter. She fought trying to get out of his grasp. He bent down on one knee hugging her tightly.

"Daddy, she's going to die, we have to save her," Susan sobbed.

"Baby, she's already gone. She just came back to save you, because *you* helped *her*. Look, Susan. Look at the window. She's gone," he said, sobbing. "Oh, Susan, look at you! You're walking! It took the love a cat for you to walk! I'm sure your Happy is at peace now, and is indeed very, very happy."

Dead Wrong

Alan sat waiting for the light to change. It was late and the traffic was the usual, heavy Friday traffic. He sat thinking about his retirement—he only had two more weeks to go. He was so tired of the heavy work load, he just wanted out. He had an uneasy feeling, the kind you get when you're walking in a dark area and you feel someone behind you, as if someone was watching. He looked over at the bus sitting beside him in the next lane. Looking up at the window of the bus he saw a man staring at him. Directly seated in front of the man was a woman staring also. They both looked familiar. He tried to recall where he had seen them before. The bus moved forward with the traffic, and soon the man and woman were out of sight.

Alan was relieved when he finally made it home. The man's staring eyes were still on his mind as he stepped into the shower. He was trying to think about where it was he had seen him before. The man and the woman both seemed so familiar. He was sure he had seen them somewhere, but where? The water pounding on his skin seemed to ease the day's problems, beating them gently from his thoughts.

He stepped into the hallway from the bathroom in his robe, feeling refreshed from the shower, rather renewed, still thinking about his retirement. It had been a long thirty years. Being the county coroner had definitely taken its toll over the years. He was more then ready to get out of the rat race. He had had his fill.

He stopped dead in his tracks as he entered the living room. In front of him, seated on his couch were the man and woman he had seen staring at him from the bus. He felt his knees weaken, as if the life was draining from him. He was terrified, too afraid to move, and wouldn't have been able to anyway. He was frozen from the fear that had taken control of his body. They both sat staring at him but said nothing. As his senses eased their way back into his drained body, he began to wonder how they had gotten in. What did they want? Were they here to rob him? Kill him? They sat in silence staring at him. Once he realized they weren't going to say anything, he forced himself to speak. "What do you want?" The words were weak and cracking, barely making their way out from his dried throat.

"Want?" The man spoke up, questioning his question. "I'll tell you what we want. Or maybe I should say *need*. Yes, need. You are getting ready to retire, right?" His words were quick and precise. How did this man know this? Maybe he worked in the hospital. Maybe he had seen him at work and overlooked him as he did several people. He wasn't good at making friends. He very rarely even spoke to the people who worked with him daily. "What we need are some documents changed," the man continued.

"Changed?" Alan replied, puzzled by what the man was asking. "Documents? What kind of documents do you mean?"

"Well, death certificates of course," the man said as he stood up from the couch. Alan had started to relax a little as the man's voice had managed to ease him some, but now with him walking toward him, he became apprehensive again. "After all, you are the coroner, right?"

"Yes, I am," Alan said, managing to get his weakened voice to answer. "But why would I want to change a death certificate? Is it for an insurance claim?"

"You think it's for an insurance claim? No, no, no, you got this all wrong." He threw his hands in the air, and shook his head as he spoke. "You see, some years back, twenty-five to be exact, you made a couple of big mistakes. As a matter of fact they happened to both be in the same weekend. Two people died that weekend and you ruled both deaths to be suicides. Well, I think that now is the time for you to change these rulings, before you retire and no longer will be able to."

"What makes you think they were mistakes? Why would I want to change them now after all this time? I would need proof anyway, you know. I can't just go changing records because some friend or family member wants me to."

"We have your proof." The woman, having been quiet all this time, spoke up, her shrilling voice cutting through the silence like a piece of chalk against a blackboard. "Proof … is that what you want? We are not family members, or even friends of the victims. No, that isn't it at all." She stood up and walked over to stand next to the man standing in front of Alan. "No, Mr. Rickell," she said startling Alan as she said his name. "You see, we are the victims."

"Victims," he said as his eyes darted back and forth between the two people that were standing before him. "How are you the victims? You would have to be dead. Wouldn't you?"

The man motioned toward the couch. "Maybe you had better sit down, Alan." He said in a soothing voice. "And we'll tell you just what we are really doing here."

Alan walked over to the couch. He felt like he was dreaming. Was this really happening? His body didn't seem to respond to do what he wanted it to do, which was to get out of the apartment and away from these people—but it responded well to what the man suggested. He sat down on the couch and looked at the man and woman who had followed him and had seated themselves one on each side of him.

"Alright now," the man said with serious concern covering his face, as he looked at Alan. "I'll try to explain the nature of our visit for you. About twenty-five years ago, just a few years after you started as coroner, there were a couple of deaths in this county. You ruled them both as suicide." Alan started to speak but was silenced by the man holding his hand up to stop him as he continued with his story. "The rulings went unquestioned and were unjustified on both counts. We were both killed in the same weekend, in the same county, and were both ruled as suicide. This is what has bound us together for all these years. We have tried to put information in front of you, and even questioned you at various times about the deaths, but you would always say you would have to check your records. But that never happened. Did it?"

Alan thought the two had looked familiar, now he knew why. He remembered seeing them from time to time in press conferences. Now he remembered them always bringing up the two incidents. He had thought that maybe they were family members trying to clear the records. He knew the records were dubbed to sound more efficient, that was how things were done in his earlier days as coroner. No one had ever questioned his findings—that is, no one until now.

"First let us introduce ourselves," the man continued. "I am Bob Strider, and this is Mary Jensen. Would you like to start first, Mary?" he asked, motioning toward the woman. Alan looked at her. She was a nice-looking woman, tall and slim with her unkempt, long, shaggy, blonde curls draping her shoulders. Her large, sad eyes seemed ready to burst forth with a flood of tears at any moment. She nodded her head and looked directly at Alan as she hesitated, searching for the words to tell her story in the proper perspective.

"I was so much in love," she started, her voice cracking as she fought to keep back the tears. "I was going to elope that weekend with my boyfriend, Jeff. I had been sneaking around to see him. My father and brother would never allow me to have a boyfriend. They would never allow me to hardly have any friends at all. They wanted me there to clean up after them and wait on them hand and foot. I met Jeff at a friend's house, one of the few friends I was allowed to have. Our first meeting was something like in the story books. From the beginning, we knew we were meant for each other. We would see each other as often as we could. My friend started giving us precious, private time together. I'll never forget the first time we made love. He was so gentle, so caring, like nothing I could have ever imagined a man to be like, not after having been with the likes of my drunken father. Yes, he raped me every time he would feel the need. He said I was his to do with as he pleased. I was afraid to tell Jeff about my father, afraid he would leave me, or maybe kill him and be locked away for life. But I became pregnant. I really didn't know who the baby belonged to, but I knew I had to tell Jeff, because if my father found out he would have beat me for sure, and would probably have caused me to lose the baby. When I told Jeff, he was furious. I begged him to stay away from my father. I told him I didn't want to lose him to a jail, but if he wanted to leave, I would understand. He told me he was coming for me the following weekend, and we would go to Indian Lake and get married. He told me to pack lightly, but to take what I didn't want to part with, because I wasn't coming back.

We planned to meet at the old abandoned farm house on our property. I knew that Saturday my father and brother would go to town with their buddies and wouldn't be back until late. That Saturday, as soon as they left, I packed my few, precious belongings in a brown paper bag, and went to the farm house to wait for Jeff. I waited for hours in that house. What I never knew was that Jeff was in an accident on his way there. I figured something was wrong. I thought that maybe he had had car trouble. Not once though did I think that he had changed his mind and had backed out. No, that wasn't at all like him. I knew he would be there as soon as possible. What I didn't count on, however, was my brother coming home early. When he didn't find me in the house he became worried, not that something had happened to me, but that I had run away. When he opened the front door, Blue Bell, our old hound dog, darted out the door and headed for the old farm house. My brother jumped in his truck and followed. I could hear Blue bellowing outside the door, the way she would whenever she would tree a coon. I couldn't remember whether she had been outside or inside when I left, but when I heard my brother pull up in his pick-up, I figured out what had happened, and knew that Blue Bell had led him to me. I looked for a place to hide, but knew that hiding downstairs was out of the question, because of Blue, so I grabbed my sack with my things and hurried up the rickety steps of the house and pulled down the loft ladder to the attic. I pulled the ladder back up and closed the loft door, but didn't think to pull the rope up.

When my brother got out of his truck, seeing how Blue was acting, he grabbed his shotgun from the rack behind his seat. When he came in the house, he called out my name but I kept quiet. Blue went bellowing through the house and right up the stairs and stood under the attic opening, looking up and howling for all she was worth. I heard my brother climbing the stairs slowly. He wasn't sure if I was alone or not. He stood under the attic and kept calling to me asking if I was up there or not. He hollered up saying there had better not be anyone with me, as he pulled the ladder down with the rope that I had left hanging. When he opened the trapdoor I was crouched in a corner of the attic, the darkest corner I could find. It was fairly dark but the windows had been broken out allowing some light from the fading day to filter into the room. He saw me crouched, hiding in the shadows. 'What do you think you are doing up here?' he yelled. He had his gun ready to use as he searched the shadows for another person. As he looked around, he spotted my bag. 'What's this?' he screamed at me, kicking my bag causing my things to spill out onto the dirty wooden floor. 'What do you think you're doing, running away or something?' he raved. 'You just wait until Pa gets a hold of you.' I sat there watching my dreams drift away. I didn't care anymore about myself, but I was afraid that Jeff would pull up at any time. 'I'm not going back,' I told him. There were tears on my face but I could feel the anger swelling inside my stomach. 'You and that dirty, old man can make it on your own. You're not using me anymore!' 'Well, we'll just see about that!' he yelled as he reached down and grabbed me by my hair, pulling me across the floor. He was walking backwards and wasn't watching where he was stepping. He hit a loose board in the floor and fell backwards. I heard the loud crack of the gun being fired as he went down. I felt like someone had hit me in the face with a flaming hot skillet. The unbearable heat flashed through my head but the pain only lasted a few short seconds, then I felt numb and everything turned dark.

My brother left the house with the gun still in his hands, then drove to town to pick up my father. After he told him what had happened, they both returned to the house. My father was really upset, but not because he had killed me, but because he had left with the gun. He kept hollering about what a fool he was as he wiped the gun off and put it close to my hand to make it look like I had done it myself. So you see, Mr. Rickell, that is what really happened," she said seeing the sorrowful concern that had covered the eyes she had been staring in. "It's not that I have any real reason for clearing this up. There is no one I have to please other than my good friend who introduced me to Jeff. I guess it's only to set the record straight. I know it was an accident, it was just the way they handled it, and their lack of concern, I guess that was what made me want revenge. But you know what is really ironic?" she asked but answered herself before Alan could open his mouth. "The person I had planned to meet that day, who my father and brother had thought they kept me from meeting—I still met him that day. You see, he was killed in the wreck he was in. He was there to meet me when I died and passed over. We are not together yet though. I need to get this incident cleared up first, and then we will be together."

"But how was I to know? I mean all signs pointed to suicide," Alan said, burying his face in his hands.

"All signs, Mr. Rickell? No! No signs pointed to suicide. Think back. There was no investigation. You were in a hurry, remember? You were getting ready to go on vacation, and you already had a previous death to deal with from earlier the same day: Bob's, which was also botched for obvious reasons. Since this was also an election year, you didn't want any unsolved murder cases on your agenda. Did you? So if you had investigated, you would have found the drag marks in the dust, on the floor where my brother had dragged me, which would have told you there was someone else there. Also, there were no prints on the gun, not even mine, or blood splatters either, which would show the gun had been wiped clean—but since there was no investigation, you never knew that did you? And what was I doing with my brother's gun? Everyone knew he always carried it in his truck. I'm sure someone saw it that day, but you never had it checked out. It was so much easier to rule it a suicide. Wasn't it?"

"Yes it was so much easier, wasn't it Alan?" Bob said, drawing Alan's attention to him. "But unlike Mary here, I had a family who the suicide ruling affected. Let me tell you about your first case that day." He shifted himself on the couch in a position so that he was facing Alan more directly as he spoke.

"As I came home from work the night before, I stopped by the bank to cash my check; it was payday. Plus it was even a larger payday for me because that day I had cashed in some bonds, you see I needed to get the kids some school clothes that weekend, because school was going to start the following Wednesday. So you see, when I got home I had over five hundred dollars on me. When I arrived at home, my wife wasn't there yet, so I fixed the kids' supper for them. She came home a couple of hours after we had eaten, and we started arguing about what I had fixed and why I didn't wait on her to get home. I drank a lot in those days. My friends were always at the bar, so if I wanted to see them that is where I would go and I most always ended up having too much to drink. A lot of times I would walk home, but usually on Friday nights, someone would take me. If you tried to walk home on Friday nights the police were right there to pick you up, and make you pay them to keep them from taking you to jail. It was usually twenty five dollars, but that was a lot back then. Anyway, I had quite a bit to drink that night and left the bar when my cousin left; he drove me home. I staggered in the house feeling pretty good from the alcohol racing through my blood. I didn't notice my daughter lying in the bed with my wife as I sat down to pull my shoes off, and I sat on her causing her to wake up. My wife hollered at me and told me to leave, so I left and walked back to the bar and I stayed this time until it closed. The police picked me up as I was walking up the street on the way home again. It was officers Damian and Shagan. They wanted their pay, the usual twenty five dollars—until I pulled out my wallet and they saw how much money I really had. They took my wallet and pulled out the money and counted it. I had five hundred fifty five dollars left.

'Where did you get all this money Bob?' Officer Damian asked me. 'You robbed a bank or what?' I told him I had cashed in some bonds to get some things for the house and the kid's school clothes. He looked at officer Shagan who was driving and said, 'what do you think, do you think we should let him have any of this back?'

Shagan said not to give me back the money. Said I would just drink it up and besides—his kids needed school clothes too. I told him he wasn't going to keep my money, he could take me to jail if he wanted, but he wasn't going to keep it. They pulled through the alley that was facing the back of my house and stopped the car and got out. Officer Damian opened the door and dragged me out. 'Come on Bob, you're sleeping in the barn tonight,' he said as he grabbed my arms and pulled them behind me. I tried to push away from him but I was too intoxicated and he was too strong. He told me I was going to keep quiet about this as he headed me in the direction of the barn. I don't know if it was the amount I had to drink or my stubbornness that made me come back at them. But something put a fight in me. I kicked my leg behind me, kicking Shagan in the shin and causing him to loosen his hold on me. Then Damian grabbed me by the front of my shirt and spun me around. He drew back his fist to hit me. I knew they were going to beat me but I had to get at least one thing in before they did, so I spit in Damian's face. I saw the rage form in his eyes, as his fist made contact with my jaw, knocking me to the ground. He immediately jumped on top of me with his hands around my throat, choking me. I couldn't breath, I felt myself fading, and then everything went black. But the funny thing was, I could still hear their voices. I heard Shagan in a hoarse half-whisper saying, 'Come on, Damian, get off him. Oh my God, I think you killed him.'

'Well, you saw what he did, didn't you?' Damian said as he stood up, brushing himself off. 'He spit in my face. Nobody spits in my face and gets away with it.' He looked down at me and kicked at my limp body. 'Yeah, oh my God, I think he is dead! What are we going to do?'

Shagan reached down and grabbed one of my arms and legs. 'Come on; let's get him in the barn,' he said to Damian. Then they carried my body to the barn and dropped me on the dirt floor.

'We've got to make this look like a suicide,' Shagan said. 'I don't know how many times his wife has called the station saying he was going to kill himself, so this should easily work. First we'll need some rope.'

'I saw a rope swing on that tree in the back yard,' Damian stated as the sweat poured down his face. He knew he had to do whatever it took to get himself out of this foul up.

'Good, you got a knife on you?' Shagan asked as Damian shook his head for an answer. 'That's alright,' he said, 'I'll get one from the house. It shouldn't be too hard to get in.' He left the barn, and Damian paced back and forth looking at me as he waited for Shagan to return. It wasn't long before he returned, carrying the rope from the swing. They made a noose, threw the rope over a rafter and tied it off. It took both of them to lift my body high enough to place the noose over my head. They let go of me causing the rope to tighten around my neck from the weight of my body pulling it as I swung back and forth. Suddenly, I woke up and grabbed at the rope around my neck, but I was too weak to help myself and the struggling didn't last long. I could hear Damian's voice as my life faded away. 'Oh my God,' he whispered loudly, 'he was still alive!' They placed my empty wallet in my back pocket and left. My kids were the ones who found me the next morning." He looked at Alan who was holding his face in his hands rubbing his forehead. "So you see, Alan, an investigation would have shown that I couldn't have possibly hung myself. There was nothing I could have stood on, besides the wash tub that was leaning against the wall, but the tub would have left a ring in the dirt, and there was no ring. I'm sure that you had to have seen the bruises on my neck caused from Officer Damian choking me, but it was easier for you to call it a suicide, wasn't it? And it was my family who had to pay for that judgment."

Alan rubbed his face and looked at Bob. "I'm really sorry," he said. "But it's too late to do anything now. I mean twenty-five years causes things to be forgotten. Nobody really cares anymore what happened back then."

"You mean you're not going to try to clear the record?" Bob asked as he stood up.

"It would really be a waste of time," Alan said shaking his head. "I don't have that kind of time. I mean, I retire in two weeks, and it would take longer than that to find those old records, if they even still exist. We had a fire fifteen years back that destroyed a lot of the records. Then also it would be up to the new coroner to consider whether changing the records would be worthwhile or justifiable. I think it's best to leave the past alone."

Bob reached down and took Mary by the hand. "It's time for us to leave, Mary," he said. "We've done all we can do here." They walked across the floor toward the door; they stopped before they reached the door and turned to look back at Alan, who was still sitting dumbfounded on the couch. "It's all in your hands, Alan," Bob said, his voice void of the emotion that rang through it only minutes earlier. "Guess you made your decision."

Alan looked at Bob and Mary who were starting to fade from his sight, and he watched as their misty bodies evaporated into thin air.

Suddenly Alan was in total darkness. He tried to open his eyes but for some reason his eyelids seemed abnormally heavy. He forced open his tired eyes. He was lying on the couch. Had he been sleeping? He glanced at the clock on the mantle above the fireplace; it was hard for him to see it clearly, but he knew it was early morning. Why was he so tired? He recalled the night's occurrences and wondered if he had only been dreaming. Had he really been visited by ghosts? He tried to pull himself up but his body wouldn't respond to his wants. He couldn't move. His eyes hurt and what was that smell? Was it gas? Yes. Yes, it was gas; he knew the kitchen stove must have gotten turned on. He needed to get up and get some fresh air, but he was too tired. He was so … tired. He closed his eyes and drifted off.

The evening paper caught the attention of a few eyes, carrying the headline: **County Coroner Commits Suicide!**

012009c